Did Daniel think that was part of the babysitting package? Sydney had to admit, it would be one heck of a job perk, but even if she was in the market for a fling, it would never be with a man like him. He was way out of her league.

"I'm wondering why you're so nervous around me."

"I'm nervous around cops."

"But you know I'm a good cop. Because if you didn't, you never would have agreed to watch April. And you only get nervous when I get close, or do something like this." His fingers brushed her earlobe.

"Stop that!" she said, batting his hand away.

He grinned, and if it wasn't so damned adorable, she probably would have decked him.

"I rest my case," he said, looking pleased with himself.

Dear Reader,

Words cannot express how thrilled I am to be a new addition to the Harlequin Superromance family. It's given me the opportunity to share the story of two people who have been living in my head for a very long time.

I first "met" Sydney and Daniel in the late 1990s. Their story was one of the first full-length romantic novels I ever finished. I'll admit that the writing left a lot to be desired, but there was something special about the characters. But as is the case with first books, they were filed away, and though I tried to forget them and concentrate on new stories and characters, they would occasionally pop back into my head, demanding revisions. I could never resist giving them one last chance to shine. In a way, I felt I owed it to them, and they've taught me a lot over the years.

Their story has changed considerably with every rewrite, and they have developed as people in ways that both surprised and delighted me, but deep down they're still the same two characters who popped into my head and refused to leave me alone until I got their story right!

I always hoped that someday I would have the chance to introduce them to my readers, and here they finally are! I hope you enjoy them as much as I have.

Best,

Michelle Celmer

Nanny Next Door
Michelle Celmer

TORONTO • NEW YORK • LONDON
AMSTERDAM • PARIS • SYDNEY • HAMBURG
STOCKHOLM • ATHENS • TOKYO • MILAN • MADRID
PRAGUE • WARSAW • BUDAPEST • AUCKLAND

Recycling programs
for this product may
not exist in your area.

ISBN-13: 978-0-373-71685-2

NANNY NEXT DOOR

Printed in U.S.A.

ABOUT THE AUTHOR

USA TODAY bestselling author Michelle Celmer lives in southeastern Michigan with her husband, their three children, two dogs and two cats. When she's not writing or busy being a mom, you can find her in the garden or curled up with a romance novel. And if you twist her arm really hard, you can usually persuade her into a day of power shopping. Michelle loves to hear from readers. Visit her website, www.michellecelmer.com, or write her at P.O. Box 300, Clawson, MI 48017.

Books by Michelle Celmer

To Beppie and Geoff,
for many evenings of good food, lots of laughs,
and tales of ever-shortening skirts.

We love you guys!

CHAPTER ONE

SYDNEY HARRIS ran a finger over the dent in the kitchen wall next to the side door. The dent from the coffee cup she'd lobbed there after she'd spent a miserable night in the local lockup—thanks to her corrupt, narcissistic, creep of an ex-husband. At the time she'd considered that dent a symbol, a reminder that things could only get better, so she'd left it there. Except things hadn't gotten better. In fact, they'd gotten worse, and after today, every time she looked at that dent, she would remember the day her career went down the toilet.

"Sydney, are you still there?"

She tightened her grip on the phone. "You're firing me?" she asked Doreen Catalano, director of Meadow Ridge Early Learning Center. Her now former employer.

Her now former best friend.

"Technically, this isn't a termination. We're simply not renewing your contract. We're within the legal parameters of your employment agreement."

"Legal parameters? What about loyalty? What about the fact that we've been friends for ten years?" She applied pressure to the center of the dent and her finger popped through the drywall. Wonderful. Now there was a hole. Kind of like the rest of her life. One big gaping hole—no husband, no friends, no job. What else could she lose?

No, Syd, don't even go there.

"Call it whatever you want," she told Doreen. "I'm still out of a job."

"Sydney, you're a wonderful teacher, but you know as well as I do that we can't ignore the concerns of the parents. The rumors…"

"Will you at least write me a recommendation?" she asked. "I think you owe me that much."

After several seconds passed and Doreen didn't answer, the last of Sydney's hope sank somewhere south of her toes. "I'll take that as a *no*."

"If we were to write you a recommendation and something were to…happen…we just can't take that kind of risk. You'll receive the rest of your vacation pay and a generous severance."

If something were to *happen?* Sydney's voice shook with anger. "Forgive me if I sound ungrateful, but that hardly softens the blow. You were there, you know how much I had to drink—one lousy glass of wine at dinner. As did you, I might add, and I don't see you losing your job over it."

"I wasn't arrested for a DUI."

"I guess it doesn't count that they dropped the charges. And excuse me, but in ten years have you ever known me to be a raging alcoholic? Did I ever once show up late for work, or hungover—or intoxicated? This is all about Jeff getting revenge."

"He's the mayor. People trust him."

More like people feared him. It was obvious Doreen

did. "Let me guess. Did he threaten to have the school investigated? Maybe he said there would be trumped-up abuse charges if you didn't fire me? Did he say he would have the school's license yanked?"

There was a pregnant pause, and Sydney knew she was right. That manipulative, egotistical *bastard*. She could sue them, but frankly, she'd spent enough time in court this past year. And why would she want to teach at a school where no one trusted her?

"Sydney, maybe…well, maybe you should consider relocating. Getting a fresh start somewhere new."

No way. "I'm not running away. Prospect is my home. I won't let him steal that from me, too."

"I have your personal effects from your desk and your check if you'd like to pick them up today. This is for the best, Sydney."

"Best for whom?"

Doreen didn't answer, but Sydney had heard enough anyway. She punched the disconnect button and tossed the phone down on the counter. Nothing would change Doreen's mind, and begging wasn't an option. Not if she planned to maintain at least a shred of her dignity.

The satisfaction of raking Jeff over the coals in the divorce had been short lived when he'd set out to systematically destroy her reputation—and had now succeeded. If he heard that she'd begged for her job, and failed, he would never let her live it down. She wouldn't give him the pleasure.

She had honestly thought this mess would blow over and everything would go back to normal. She thought people knew her better than this.

Apparently, she thought wrong. Either that or people were just too afraid of her ex to cross him.

Even though Sydney had spent the past sixteen years of her life in Prospect, California, after the divorce she had been deemed an outsider. No more significant than the thousands of tourists who visited every year.

"Legal parameters, my foot," she mumbled, poking at the hole in the wall. Bits of drywall broke off, leaving a dusty white pile on the floor. It was time to patch this up and move on. To stop living in the past.

Rummaging through the kitchen drawers for something—*anything*—to cover it, Sydney settled on a roll of duct tape. It would have to do until she could buy a putty knife and spackling. She pulled off a length, tearing it with her teeth, and smoothed it over the hole. Not great, but better. Now, if she could just use the tape to temporarily repair her life.

"*Gawd,* what are you doing do to the wall?"

Sydney turned to see Lacey, her fifteen-year-old daughter, standing in the kitchen doorway. She should have left for school over an hour ago. "I was fixing a hole."

"With tape? It looks dumb."

She had to admit it did look pretty dumb. She tore the tape off, taking another chunk of drywall along with it. "You're late again."

"I overslept." Lacey shuffled into the kitchen and Sydney cringed when she noticed the latest condition of her hair—pale blond and freshly streaked in varying shades of purple. Her makeup wasn't much better. Thick black eyeliner reduced her eyes to two narrow slits, creating the illusion that she was perpetually pissed off—which, come to think of it, she was. Mauve lipstick added a touch of obstinacy, perfecting that "rebellious teen" look she worked so hard to achieve. Even her school uniform was a wrinkled mess.

It broke Sydney's heart to see the transformation her daughter had gone through. From a somewhat happy, fairly well-adjusted teenager to Wednesday Addams gone emo. Couldn't Jeff see what his behavior was doing to his child? Didn't he care?

Of course he didn't. Jeff cared about one person— *Jeff.*

"You only have a week of school left. Could you at least *try* to get there on time?"

Lacey shrugged. "Who called?"

If she could shelter Lacey from the truth, she would have. The kid had been through so much already. All she could do now was try to minimize the damage. "Doreen Catalano, from the preschool. They'll be replacing me now that my contract is up."

Lacey's mouth dropped open. "They *fired* you?"

Sydney kept her voice even. "No. They just chose not to renew my contract."

Lacey wasn't buying the calm act. "He did this, didn't he? Dad is screwing with you again."

"It's not a big deal." Sydney forced a smile. "Really. I'll find another job." *And won't that be fun without references,* she thought. Ten years of experience down the toilet. But she would manage. God knows she had overcome worse. And on the bright side, Jeff paid so much in alimony and child support, technically she didn't *need* a job. She would just have to tighten the belt a little.

They would be fine.

"I wish he would leave us alone." Lacey poured herself coffee and dumped half a cup of sugar into her mug. "I wish he would marry that bimbo and forget we exist."

Sydney suppressed a rueful smile. "Lacey, honey, please don't call your father's girlfriend a bimbo."

"Mom, she's, like, only a few years older than me. Do you have any idea how embarrassing that is?"

Seven years, actually, but who was counting? And of course Lacey was bitter. Her father's infidelities had hardly been a secret. But the last time, with his "bimbo" assistant, Sydney had had enough. She wished she could have seen his face when he'd been served with the divorce papers. And though he'd put her through hell this past year, she was still glad she did it. She was relieved to finally be free.

She gave Lacey's shoulder a squeeze. "I have to go pick up my final check. I could drop you off at school on the way."

Lacey shrugged out of reach. "No, I'll walk. I'll be home late today. I'm going to Shane's house to study for Spanish finals."

"You don't take Spanish."

She rolled her eyes. "*Duh*. I'm helping *Shane* study."

Sydney forced herself to take a deep breath and count to ten. *She's still adjusting,* that rational inner voice reminded her. *Give her time.*

"I expect you home by six," she said.

"But—"

Sydney held up a hand to shush her. "Don't bother arguing. You know your father is coming to get you for dinner."

Lacey's eyes narrowed until they all but disappeared. "I don't want to see him."

"I know you don't, and I understand why, but no matter how angry you are or how unfair all of this seems, he's still your father and he has a right to see you."

"*Fine.* What do you care if I'm psychologically scarred for the rest of my life!" She yanked her backpack off the kitchen table and stormed out the side door, slamming it behind her.

Sydney sighed, wishing there was something she could do to make this easier on her daughter. She had suggested to Jeff that they take her to see a counselor, but he refused. He didn't want people to put a label on Lacey, or so he claimed, but she was sure it was more about people labeling him a bad father. Either way, without his consent, her hands were tied. She could sue for the right, but another lengthy court battle would only make things worse.

She grabbed her car keys from the crystal candy dish on the counter, shoved her feet into her flip-flops and stepped out the side door into the late morning sun. In the distance a grayish haze ringed the crest of the Scott Bar mountains so she knew it was going to be a warm and sticky afternoon.

A thick wave of heat enveloped her as she opened

the door to her minivan, and as she climbed in she noticed that the new tenants appeared to have settled into the rental house next door. Yesterday there had been a moving van and now there was a red pickup truck in the drive. There was also an unmarked police car parked out front. She hoped that didn't mean there was going to be trouble with the new neighbors.

The previous resident, Mr. Bellevue, had been moved into an assisted living facility last month after he'd forgotten to turn off the stove and almost burned down the house for the fourth time in month.

Sydney made a mental note to stop on her way home and pick up a housewarming gift.

Pulling out of her driveway and around the police car, she started driving toward the preschool, but had barely gone fifty feet when she glanced down at the passenger seat and realized she hadn't brought her purse. No purse, no ID.

Ugh! Could this day get any worse?

She slammed on the brakes, threw the van into reverse and floored it. A blur of black in the rearview mirror made her jerk to a stop, but not before she felt the impact and heard the unmistakable crunch of glass.

And just like that, her day got worse.

Jamming the van into park, she let her head fall against the steering wheel.

Just what she needed. Another run-in with the Prospect County Sheriff's Department. One more reason for them to harass her.

She took one long, shaky breath, and with trembling

hands pushed the door open and climbed out of the van. She circled around back to check the damage.

A dented bumper and obliterated taillight on her van—that wasn't so bad. Besides a broken headlight, the police car didn't have a scratch on it. So why did she feel like throwing herself down on the pavement and sobbing? Maybe she could just leave a note on the windshield and skulk away.

Just as she'd completed the thought, she heard a door creak open and turned to see a man walking toward her from the house next door. He wore faded jeans and a sleeveless T-shirt, but she recognized him as one of Prospect's finest. Deputy Daniel Valenzia, or as she had often heard him called, Deputy Casanova. He was a confirmed bachelor and notorious breaker of female hearts all over town.

There was a time when Sydney had also been seduced by a man with authority. The only problem with authoritative men, she'd learned, was that they abused that power for selfish reasons.

She was guessing by the lack of uniform, rumpled dark hair and several days' worth of dark stubble, Deputy Valenzia wasn't here on business. He wasn't part of Jeff's lynch gang, so Sydney had never actually met him, but cops were cops as far as she was concerned. It was sad, really, because before the divorce she'd had tremendous respect for law enforcement. Now if she saw a patrol car headed her way, she pulled down the nearest side street or into the closest parking lot. A couple dozen tickets—for things as ridiculous as dirt on her license plate, not to mention a baseless arrest for DUI—could make a woman a little paranoid. Being hauled away in handcuffs on Main Street on a busy Friday night in front of half the town and twice that many tourists had been the most humiliating experience in her life by far.

Deputy Valenzia stopped a few feet from her to inspect the damage, his face unreadable. Sydney waited for the explosion, for him to berate her for her stupidity. To call her a careless woman driver. When he finally met her eyes, she was jolted with awareness.

Set over a pair of amazingly high cheekbones—cheekbones any woman would sell her soul for—his eyes were black as tar and so bottomless she felt as if she were swimming in them. And…warm? A little amused even, which made no sense at all.

Why wasn't he screaming at her? Why wasn't he ranting and raving? If it had been Jeff's BMW damaged in a fender bender, he'd have chewed the poor driver to shreds by now with harsh words and legal threats.

"So, what happened here?" he finally asked.

"I'm very sorry," she said. *I'm very sorry?* Lame, Syd, lame.

Valenzia just nodded, his eyes still locked on hers, as if he expected her to say something else. Or maybe he was checking to see if her pupils were dilated.

"I didn't mean to hit it," she said, and the second the words left her mouth, she cringed. *That's a good one,* she thought, realizing how dumb that sounded. People didn't usually *mean* to hit anything, and if they did, they didn't admit it. And what had her lawyer told her? Never give more information than asked for, and when they do ask, only give them the basic facts. Never elaborate.

Police had a way of tripping people up and making them say more than they meant to, or even things they didn't mean.

Deputy Valenzia looked at her van, then back to his car, rubbing a hand across his rough jaw. "I have to ask, how exactly did you hit the front of the car with the back of your van?"

"I was, um, backing up."

One eyebrow quirked up and she could swear she saw another glint of amusement play across his chiseled features. It was unbelievably sexy. And the fact that she thought so was unbelievably *wrong*. Just because he wasn't one of Jeff's men, it didn't mean he wasn't a bad cop.

"You make a habit of driving around the neighborhood in reverse?" he asked, the corner of his mouth twitching.

"I was going home," she said, hitching a thumb over her shoulder to indicate her house. "I forgot something." She didn't mention *what* she'd forgotten, because then he would probably cite her for operating a vehicle without a license. It would never hold up, but having to actually go to traffic court was a huge inconvenience. She'd found that if it wasn't a moving violation that would ultimately affect her driving record, it was easier just to pay the ticket and be done with it.

"You have insurance?" he asked.

"Of course." Did he think she was irresponsible?

He shrugged and pulled out a cell phone. "You never know."

Here it comes, she thought. He was going to call in

his sheriff buddies. She couldn't begin to imagine the rumors this would start. Maybe they would give her a Breathalyzer test and make her recite the alphabet backward, every third letter, just for fun.

He punched a few buttons, frowned, then banged the cell against the heel of his palm, mumbling a curse. "Phone's dead." He stuffed it back in his pocket. "Could I use yours?"

She hesitated. Wouldn't that be like bringing a gun to her own execution?

"Come on," he coaxed, giving her a lazy smile that revealed a neat row of white teeth. "It's the least you can do."

"Umm…"

"If you're worried about your safety, I'm harmless," he assured her. "I'm a cop."

Hence the cop car. If she told him no, would she look like she had something to hide? It's not as if there were no other phones in town. In fact, she was surprised he didn't just call it in on the car radio.

But maybe if she cooperated he would go easy on her. "Sure, you can use my phone."

"I'll need your insurance information, too."

"It's inside."

He gestured to her house. "After you."

She walked up the driveway, acutely aware of him behind her. She could only hope her butt didn't look as huge as it felt. As if he would even be looking at it. When they approached the side door he reached around her to open it. At least he had decent manners.

"Nice place," he said as they stepped through the door.

Not nearly as nice as the family estate she'd lived in with Jeff, but appearances had never mattered much to her. A modest three-bedroom, two-bath Cape Cod, this house suited her and Lacey just fine. And though it was older, like the house she'd grown up in back in Michigan, it had character, not to mention almost half an acre of land. And the best part was that it was all hers.

"The phone is on the counter," she said, and as Deputy Valenzia brushed past, his bare arm grazed hers, making her breath catch. The sheer energy of his presence seemed to somehow shrink the room to the size of a closet. He could have been standing fifty feet away and he would still have been too close.

With sudden alarm she wondered if maybe he wasn't as harmless as he seemed? What if he did work for Jeff and, now that he had her alone, planned to harass her? Or something worse. Who would people believe? A respected officer of the law, or the local lush?

"Proof of insurance?" he asked.

She grabbed her purse and dug through her wallet for her insurance card, aware that her hands were trembling again. She held it out to him, clutching the purse to her chest like a shield. He just stared at her for a moment and she could swear she saw that hint of amusement again in the slight lift of his brow. Did he think this was funny?

"Everything okay?" he asked.

"Of course."

"You look a little…tense."

In her situation, so would he. "I'm fine."

He shrugged, then reached up and took the card from her, his fingers brushing hers. She jerked her hand back, as though she'd touched a hot oven.

He gave her a look that said he might be questioning her mental stability. "Thanks, I'll just be a minute."

He dialed and leaned himself against the edge of her kitchen counter, crossing long muscular legs at the ankles. His jeans were tattered to the point of indecency and his T-shirt, in addition to having had both sleeves torn off, was faded black and emblazoned with the state seal.

And he was *big*. At least six-one, maybe even taller, and at five-three, she felt like a midget.

Sydney stayed close to the door—just in case she had to make a run for it—clutching her purse to her chest. Maybe she was overreacting. Absolutely nothing in his stance suggested he was about to pounce. In fact, he seemed totally relaxed.

But the way he stared at her with those dark, dark eyes, it was as though he could see right through her. Maybe it was a cop thing. Or maybe, playboy that he was, he was checking her out.

Sure he is, Syd. A gorgeous man like him looking at a woman like you.

Not that she didn't consider herself attractive. She was, in an unrefined way. Makeup, though she'd tried every subtle technique known to man, made her look cheap and her wild red hair never cooperated when she attempted the latest sleek, sophisticated style. Most days it ended up in an unruly mass of curls pulled back in a ponytail or wrestled into a clip.

And clothes? That was another disaster. She wore conservative skirts and blouses to work, but otherwise had the fashion sense of a brick. She relied on her daughter for fashion tips and clothes swapping and as a result was the only thirty-four-year-old resident in all of Prospect who dressed as if she were still in high school. But she was comfortable that way. She *liked* herself that way, and all of the complaints and criticisms Jeff had dished out over the course of their marriage—and there had been a lot—hadn't broken her spirit. Though at times he'd come close.

"Hey, Margie," Deputy Valenzia said to the person on the other end of the line. "My car was hit and I have the insurance info." He paused, scowling. "Can't I fill it out the next time I come in?" The answer must have been yes because he read off Sydney's name, insurance company and policy number. Glancing up at the clock over the sink, he scowled again. "Could you just take care of it for me? I have to get back before April wakes up."

April. His latest conquest? Maybe that was her new neighbor. Great. That meant a constant police presence on the block until they broke up, which from what she'd heard, thankfully wouldn't take long. The only thing worse would be if Deputy Valenzia was living there, but her luck couldn't possibly be that lousy.

"No," he continued, sounding irritated. "I'm next door. My cell phone is dead. I think April drooled on it."

Okay, unless his girlfriend had overactive salivary glands, April had to be a dog. One never could tell though…

He rattled off what she figured was probably his badge number, thanked Margie—whoever she was—then hung up the phone and pushed away from the counter, rising to his full, intimidating height. "Thanks."

Wait a minute? That was it?

She frowned. "You're not going to call for reinforcements?"

His dark brows knit together. "For a fender bender?"

"No Breathalyzer?"

"Do you need one?"

"Of course not! I just thought—" She really needed to keep her mouth shut.

He walked toward her, his footsteps heavy on the tile floor, and Sydney stiffened again, even though it was obvious he didn't plan to arrest her. Maybe he didn't work for Jeff after all.

She took a deep breath, forcing herself to relax.

He stopped barely a foot away, towering a good ten inches over her, until she had to crane her neck to meet his eyes. He held out the insurance card for her. "Next time watch where you're going," he said.

She nodded and plucked the card from between his fingers, careful not to make contact again. God, she hoped he was only visiting next door. She didn't think she could handle the stress of knowing there was a deputy living so close, monitoring her every move.

"Thanks for the phone." He stepped past her to the door and as he was walking out he turned back, flashing her a lazy grin. "See you around, neighbor."

CHAPTER TWO

DANIEL VALENZIA managed to contain his amusement until he was out the door and on his way across the lawn to his rental. Sydney Harris needed to take a big fat chill pill. But he couldn't really blame her for being tense, considering all she'd been through the past few months.

Her sleazebag ex-husband must have done quite a number on her. Daniel had overheard a few of the mayor's henchmen bragging about how they'd been harassing her. He'd been half tempted to take his concerns to Sheriff Montgomery, but he knew that as long as Jeff Harris was mayor, no action would be taken.

Call him old-fashioned, but Daniel believed in the law and the principle of innocent until proven guilty. He also believed that what goes around comes around, and eventually the mayor would get exactly what he deserved. And who knows, maybe Mrs. Harris was getting exactly what she deserved for being stupid enough to marry a man like the mayor.

Slipping through the front door, Daniel paused. He'd been sure April would have woken from her nap by now. Rousing every fifteen minutes last night had apparently worn her out. He tiptoed down the hall and paused in front of April's room, pressing his ear to the door.

Silence.

In hindsight, he shouldn't have left her alone in the house, but he was still getting used to taking care of a baby.

He opened the door a crack and peeked into the room. The sounds of her faint, whispery breathing assured him she was still sound asleep. He should have just enough time to hop into the shower and take a long-overdue shave.

He crept down the hall to the bathroom. April, however, had some sort of supersonic baby radar, because the second his foot hit the tile floor she started to wail.

Daniel felt like banging his head against the wall. Something had to be wrong with that kid. She never slept! He just wasn't cut out for this parenting stuff. What if he screwed her up for life? April was so small and helpless and he didn't know the first thing about what an infant needed.

He hurried back down the hall to her room. She was lying on her back, fists balled up tight, legs and arms extended, face purple as she screamed bloody murder. Boy did she have a temper; just like her mother, if memory served. And yet when April wasn't screaming she was a pint-size heartbreaker.

When she looked up at him with her big blue eyes, tears rolling down her rosy cheeks, his first instinct was to do something crazy, like run out and buy her a pony. He'd always been good with kids, but usually when they were old enough to toss a football or swing a bat. Like his nephew, Jordan.

He had no idea what to do with this squirming, demanding bundle of attitude.

He lifted her up out of her crib and cuddled her to his chest, patting her warm, little back. Her lower lip quivered pathetically and her cheeks were damp with tears. She looked up at him with wide, accusing eyes, then let loose again with another round of ear-piercing screams.

"Come on, April," he coaxed, bouncing her gently. "Go back to sleep. Twenty more minutes, kiddo, that's all I'm asking for."

Things would get easier when he found a babysitter, he told himself. Which had better be soon because he'd used up all of his paid leave. The next option would be to take unpaid family leave, but he'd already blown through a chunk of his savings buying baby furniture, diapers, formula and the million other things required to properly care for an infant. She'd been dropped on his doorstep by the social worker with little more than a diaper bag with a dozen or so diapers, a few threadbare sleepers and a couple of bottles.

It was no wonder the dads on the force never seemed to have a nickel to spare.

He'd placed an ad in the paper for a sitter, and even put up a flyer at the local high school to find a kid looking for a summer job, but most high school and college students spent their summers working at the resort up the mountain. He couldn't begin to compete with the hourly rate they paid. So far the ones who had answered the ad either couldn't work the hours he needed, or were so scary he wouldn't let them within ten feet of April.

The only decent, affordable day-care center in town had a waiting list almost four months long—and he'd still need to find someone else to watch her when he worked the occasional evening or weekend shift. In the past few weeks Daniel had developed a healthy respect for the stresses a single parent faced. He'd never considered having kids, much less having one alone.

He still had no idea why April's mother listed him as the father on the birth certificate. A simple blood test would have proven the baby wasn't his. Maybe Reanne didn't know who the father was, and Daniel's name was the first to come to mind. Or maybe because he was a cop she felt he was the only person she could trust. She'd told him horror stories about growing up in foster care, being shuffled from family to family, never feeling she belonged anywhere. He could understand why she wanted better for April. But he couldn't be the one to provide that. He didn't know a damned thing about raising a baby. But when social services had contacted him after Reanne's death and he saw April, looking so tiny and helpless, he hadn't been able to turn her away.

He would take care of her until her real family could be found. He'd hired a buddy of his, a retired cop turned private investigator, to locate a relative willing to adopt her.

Daniel just had to hold on until then, and in the meantime hope he didn't scar the kid for life.

SYDNEY SMOOTHED the putty knife one last time over the newly patched wall. A little sandpaper and paint and it would be good as new.

After returning home she'd taken a long, hot shower, hoping to wash away some of the festering resentment toward her former employer. It hadn't worked. And now, as she sorted through the items lying on the table in front of her—handmade gifts from her students, class photos and keepsakes—she felt pitifully empty as well. Teaching was her life. Nothing filled her with joy like spending her day surrounded by her students.

Through the kitchen window she heard a car door slam. Then the side door flew open and the source of her troubles breezed in like he owned the place. Which he did just to annoy her, despite being warned by her lawyer that it was against the law. Law that he carried conveniently in his pocket.

Jeff's short blond hair—which without the dye would now be mostly gray—was neatly combed and sprayed into place, his dark blue Italian silk suit tailored to an impeccable fit. He never left home looking anything less than perfect.

"Get out," she told him.

"What, no kiss?" Jeff shrugged out of his jacket, draped it over the back of a kitchen chair and opened the refrigerator. "What's for lunch?"

She stood and clasped her thin silk robe snugly to her chest. He'd seen her in her robe thousands of times, but not since the divorce. It felt like an invasion of her privacy now. "There's a Taco Hut two blocks away."

"I wanted to let you know Kimberly's class was canceled and I can't take Lacey out tonight. I'll pick her up Saturday instead."

"That's what the phone is for."

"*And* I didn't think you would mind if I stopped by for a bite to eat, seeing as how I'm paying the mortgage."

"How stupid do I look?"

He glanced at her over the refrigerator door. "You don't really want me to answer that, do you?"

"You're here to gloat, admit it. Someone must have called to congratulate you by now. To let you know you've screwed me out of a job."

He pulled out a package of lunch meat, the mustard and a butter knife from the drawer, and put them on the counter. "You lost your job?" He flashed her that fake innocent look she could spot a mile away.

"Don't patronize me. Have you even thought about Lacey?"

"What about her?" He opened the pantry, searching for a loaf of bread. She slammed it shut and he yanked his hand away. "Hey! Watch the manicure."

"Haven't you noticed what this is doing to her? These mind games you're playing. Her grades have dropped, her appearance is atrocious. She's a mess."

"Maybe she'd be better off coming to live with me and Kimberly."

"*Better off?* Are you kidding? You've been a lousy father."

"Maybe you're a lousy mother. There is a nasty rumor circulating that you may not be a fit parent. What with your alcohol problem."

Her gut reaction was to snatch the butter knife off the counter and drive it repeatedly into his back. Then she considered the hassle it would be disposing of a two-hundred-pound corpse and changed her mind. Instead she put the knife back in the drawer and the lunch meat in the refrigerator. "Get out."

"Did I mention I won't be able to take Lacey out next week, either?" Jeff said. "I'm taking Kimberly to Hawaii for a few days."

He knew Sydney loved Hawaii. But if it meant never having to look at his arrogant face, she could live without their annual trip.

"We're going to the Virgin Islands next month," he added, and she clenched her teeth.

"What are you trying to do?" she asked. "Subdue her with jet lag?"

"Jealousy is so unattractive, Sydney."

She folded her arms across her chest. "I'm just curious to see how long it takes her to drain you and move on to her next victim."

His smug laugh echoed in her ears with the grating effect of nails on a chalkboard. "The only place she's draining me is in the bedroom. You can think about that while you're standing in the unemployment line."

Bastard. She should have used the butter knife when she had the chance.

"While you're here, the air-conditioning is acting up again," she told him and watched the smile disappear from his face. It frosted him that as part of the divorce settlement, not only did he have to buy her a house, but he was responsible for any maintenance and repairs as long as Lacey was a minor. One of the many benefits of having a shark for an attorney.

"I'll call someone next week."

"We can do this through our lawyers if you'd prefer."

Tight-lipped, he said, "I'll call today."

"Good. Now get the hell out of my house."

Lunch forgotten, Jeff grabbed his suit jacket and slung it over his shoulder and strode out the side door. He slammed it with such force her newly patched wall shook. She watched as the spackling came loose, fell away and landed with a splat on the floor.

LACEY SLIPPED DOWN THE HALL and into her room before her parents could see her. No way in a million years would she go live with her father and his bimbo.

Lacey hated *Kimberly* almost as much as she hated her father. The first and only time he'd taken them both out to dinner, Kimberly had looked at Lacey as if she were a bug she intended to squash. Her dad even had the nerve to suggest that his perfect little Kimberly could take her shopping for some decent clothes and teach her how to apply makeup correctly.

"Why, so I can look like a slut?" she had asked, and her father went ballistic. Now he only took her out on nights when the bimbo had class. She was learning French, or something lame like that. Lacey would run away from home and live in a Dumpster before she let some pasty-faced old judge tell her she had to go live with them.

She picked up the phone, dialing Shane's cell number.

"Yo," he answered, music blaring into her ear.

"Come get me," she whispered.

"Lacey? Is that you?" he yelled.

"Yes, it's me!" she hissed. "Turn down the music."

The music faded into the background. "Why are you whispering?"

"Come pick me up. I have to get out of here."

He hesitated. "But I just dropped you off, like, two minutes ago."

"I don't care! Come and get me, but park down at the corner. I'll meet you."

He let out a loud sigh. "Fine. I'll be right there."

She hung up and walked over to her bedroom door, peeking out into the hall. She could hear her mom in the kitchen, banging things around. She always did that when she was mad. And she'd been mad a lot lately.

Lacey crept back down the hall and out the front door, so her mom wouldn't hear her. Her father was long gone and when she reached the corner Shane was waiting.

"I thought you had to go home," he said as she climbed in.

"Not anymore." She used her cell to call her mom and tell her she would be late.

"Something came up at work and your dad can't make it tonight," her mom said.

Lacey knew it was a lie. She knew her father dumped her for the bimbo. *Again.* She had no clue why her mom always tried to protect him.

"I'll be home by ten," she said and hung up before her mom could say no.

She tossed the phone on the seat and turned on the radio, cranking up the volume. As long as the music was loud, she could forget about how messed up everything had become.

When her parents were still married and fighting constantly, she would sit in her room with the music turned up. She didn't want to hear the awful things they said to each other. She'd hoped the fighting would stop when they finally got divorced, but it had only gotten worse. Every time she saw her dad, he was meaner and meaner to her mom.

As Shane tore down the street, Lacey plucked a pack of cigarettes from his shirt pocket. He handed her a lighter and she lit them each one. She inhaled deeply, feeling the smoke burn her lungs.

Shane reached over and turned down the radio. "Okay, what did I do?"

She flicked her ashes out the open window. "What do you mean?"

"You only smoke when you're pissed off about something."

She brought her knees up to her chin and hugged her legs. "It's not you." The cigarette was starting to make her sick so she tossed it out the window. "My life sucks and it's all that bimbo's fault."

Shane huffed. "That's nothing. My dad brought home Bimbo Number Four last Saturday. I think he's getting married again."

It annoyed her that Shane always thought his problems were bigger. He didn't get it. His family was normal compared to hers. But he was cute, had a cool car and money to burn. And he didn't treat her like she was a freak. So what if he wasn't the best kisser in the world? Kissing was highly overrated as far as she was concerned. That was as far as she would let him go, anyway. No way was she going to take a chance and end up pregnant and married like her mom. She wasn't *ever* getting married.

"My mom lost her job today," Lacey told Shane, even though she was pretty sure he didn't care. "It's all my father's fault. I hate him." She turned to look out the window, squeezing her eyes shut. She wasn't going to cry. She never cried in front of anyone.

"So, what do you want to do now?" he asked.

"We've got finals to study for."

"Boring."

Typical Shane. He didn't take school seriously. Actually, there wasn't much he did take seriously. But he was right: studying was boring and she doubted she'd be able to concentrate anyway.

"Okay," she said, turning to him with a sly smile. "Let's do something fun instead. Something that will really piss my dad off."

"Great, let's do something fun."

She couldn't stop the bad stuff that was happening or change the past, but she could get back at her father for all the crap he'd put them through. And she knew just how to do it.

SYDNEY WOKE late the next morning, a blazing headache thrumming the inside of her skull. She shuffled to the kitchen, doing her best to ignore the damaged wall, and fished a can of coffee from the cupboard. She pried off the plastic lid and groaned. Empty.

Out of sheer desperation she put the kettle on to boil and dug out an ancient jar of instant decaffeinated shoved to the back on the uppermost shelf. A trace of caffeine was better than nothing. She spooned a clump of the gooey, congealed crystals into her cup, filled it with boiling water, and sipped, scrunching up her nose with distaste. It ranked right up there with the sludge left in the pot in the teachers' lounge at the end of the day.

"Why are you drinking instant coffee?" Lacey asked from behind her.

Startled, Sydney spun around, sloshing hot liquid down the front of her robe.

"Please don't sneak up on me like that!" She grabbed a sponge from the sink and dabbed up the stain. "Why aren't you at school?"

"Why are you drinking instant?" Lacey crossed her arms over her wrinkled blouse. Her hair, streaked green today, hung limply over her shoulders and looked like it could use a good washing.

Sydney dumped her coffee down the sink. "Because we ran out of the other kind."

"What am *I* supposed to drink?" she asked, as if the world revolved around her getting coffee in the morning.

"I'll stop at the market today." She dropped the jar in the recycling bin under the sink, and, turning back to her daughter, gasped. "Good God, what have you done to your face?"

"Isn't it cool?" Lacey reached up to press a finger to her slightly swollen, newly pierced eyebrow.

Breathe, Sydney. Don't kill her, just breathe. It was Lacey's way of taking control of her otherwise chaotic life. And it wasn't permanent, that was all that mattered. Although she couldn't help thinking tattoos would be next.

She tried to remain calm. "Honey, you already have ten holes in each ear. If you keep puncturing your head it's going to deflate."

Lacey rolled her eyes. "Ha-ha."

"Why aren't you in school?"

She touched her brow and cringed. "I have a headache."

Yeah, right. "Tough. Take two aspirin and get your butt to school. If you want to mutilate your body, you're going to have to live with the consequences."

"Fine," she grumbled. "I need a note for the office."

After Lacey left, Sydney showered and dressed, and because she'd forgotten to buy a gift yesterday, whipped up a quick chicken casserole to present to her new neighbor.

Call her manipulative, but if she was going to have to live next door to a cop, she might as well try to get on his good side.

Sydney stepped outside and cut across the grass to the house next door. She knocked and barely ten seconds passed before Deputy Valenzia appeared in the doorway. He hadn't shaved since yesterday, and the thick dark stubble made him look…dangerous. In her experience, most cops were.

He folded his arms across that impressively wide chest and said, "Don't tell me you hit it again."

She forced a smile and held out the casserole dish. "I brought you a housewarming gift."

He opened the door, stepping out onto the porch, and she instinctively took a step back. Holy cow, he was big. Tall and trim with just the right amount of muscle in all the right places.

Perfect.

He took the dish from her, their fingers barely brushing. There it was again, that annoying zing of awareness.

"I didn't introduce myself yesterday," he said, holding out a hand for her to shake. "Daniel Valenzia."

The absolute last thing she wanted to do was touch him, but she couldn't be rude, either.

"Sydney Harris." She slipped her hand into his and he clasped it firmly. Possessively.

It was the stupid badge he wore. That was the only reason she felt so nervous. It wasn't his rough palm against hers or the sexy grin that heated her blood. Or the fact that he seemed in no hurry to let go.

She pried her hand from his and gestured over her shoulder toward home. "Um, I should probably—" She was interrupted by the unmistakable howl of a crying baby. Deputy Valenzia had a *baby?*

No way.

"Shoot, she's awake." He yanked the door open. "Don't go anywhere. I'll be right back."

"But—"

"Give me two minutes," he called as he disappeared

into the house, then added in his cop voice, "Don't leave!"

She should have left right then, but curiosity got the best of her. Two more minutes wouldn't kill her, right?

She knew Deputy Valenzia wasn't married, so he must have been babysitting for a friend, although he didn't exactly strike her as the babysitting type. Not for an infant, anyhow.

Two minutes stretched into three and she peered inside, wondering if she should keep waiting or just leave. The baby was still wailing pitifully. Another two minutes passed and the screams increased in intensity, until the infant had worked itself into a frenzy of choking and gasping. It sounded as if the deputy needed some help, and if *he* didn't, that poor baby did. Sydney didn't typically walk uninvited into stranger's houses, especially strangers with the authority to throw her in jail, but she had to do *something*.

Her maternal instincts overwhelming her, she stepped inside. The house was smaller than hers, but cozy. A black leather sofa and matching love seat, glass-top coffee and end tables and a television on a mahogany credenza were the only furniture in the living room. Guy furniture. Dirty plates, cups, bowls and baby bottles littered every flat surface. The walls were freshly painted stark white, the hardwood floors newly polished. And it smelled like...baby powder.

She followed the screams down the hall past a small empty room, then a larger room with a mussed, king-size bed, chest of drawers and a floor covered in discarded laundry. Deputy Valenzia's bedroom, she surmised with a flutter of interest. She wondered how many women he'd taken to that bed… She probably didn't want to know. If the rumors were true, living right next door, she would see the evidence soon enough.

Feeling like a snoop, Sydney continued on to the bedroom at the end the hall and looked in. A white crib sat adjacent to a matching dresser and rocking chair, and against the far wall was a changing table. In the middle of it all Deputy Valenzia stood with the hysterical infant over his shoulder, patting her back, looking as if he might burst into tears, too.

It just might have been the sweetest thing she'd ever seen.

"Can I help?" she asked over the screams.

He didn't look angry that she'd let herself in. In fact, he seemed relieved to see her.

"She was up half the night. I don't think she likes the new house." He awkwardly shifted the baby to the opposite shoulder and patted her back. Sydney had never seen a man who moved with such natural ease look so uncoordinated holding a baby. It was unbelievably cute.

"Change is difficult for young children," she said, stepping tentatively into the room. "They're creatures of habit."

The baby whimpered against his shoulder, then lifted her head and wailed again—and Sydney's heart melted. The child's plump red cheeks were dotted with tears, her clear blue eyes wide and accusing.

"Oh, she's beautiful," Sydney breathed. "How old?"

"Five months."

She held out her arms. "Let me try."

"You have experience with babies?" he asked, extending a protective hand across the child's back.

"I worked in day care all through college, taught school for ten years and I have a daughter who suffered a severe case of colic," Sydney said. "Though I still say she's more trouble as a teenager."

"That's good enough for me." He thrust the squirming, noisy bundle into Sydney's arms. "This is April. She's all yours."

CHAPTER THREE

"Oh, so you're April." Sydney held the baby up to get a good look at her. "I thought you were a puppy."

"A puppy?" Daniel asked.

"Yesterday you said April drooled on your cell phone so I assumed she was a dog."

"A puppy couldn't be much more destructive. She puts everything in her mouth."

He watched as his new neighbor laid the baby against her shoulder, rubbing her back. Sydney wasn't beautiful in the conventional sense, but there was something about her, something that appealed to him. The eyes that were a little too round, the slightly upturned nose that was too cute to belong to a mature woman, and the sprinkling of freckles across her cheeks that made her look twelve. Although, he was guessing she was probably only a few years younger than him.

She wasn't wearing much makeup, although she was attractive enough without it. Her hair was twisted up and fastened in a large clip. The loose wavy strands falling out from every direction gave her a natural, unspoiled appearance—bordering on wild and unruly. He tried to picture her prim and proper in the typical teacher wardrobe, but the only image he could conjure up was one of her sitting in a field of wildflowers, a chain of daisies around her head, holding her fingers up in a peace sign.

She cradled April against her bosom, which Daniel couldn't help but admire, and the baby instantly quieted. If he were nestled against her breasts he wouldn't be complaining, either.

Yeah, right, as if *that* would ever happen. As if his life wasn't complicated enough. He had a strict rule of never dating a single mom. Or a next-door neighbor. He tended to stay clear of divorcees, too.

"Her belly is tight," Sydney said.

Daniel's pulse skipped, his first thought being cysts or tumors or ruptured embolisms—proof he'd been watching too many hours of The Learning Channel all those late nights he'd spent pacing the floor, trying to get April to sleep. "Is that bad?"

"She probably has a gas bubble to work loose. Can I sit with her on the couch?"

"Sure." He led Sydney back to the living room. Gas he could deal with. He'd even grown accustomed to changing diapers, including the messier variety, when the stuff wouldn't stay *in* the diaper.

Sydney sat April on her lap facing Daniel and, supporting the baby's chest and neck, gently rocked her back and forth. Within seconds April stopped fidgeting and her plump little body relaxed. His new neighbor definitely had a way with babies. Why couldn't he find someone like this to babysit?

He'd received three calls that morning. Two were from college students and neither willing to work even close to the hours he needed. The other was from Margie at the station, with a message from his boss wondering when he would be back to work. If Daniel didn't find a sitter by Monday, it could mean his job.

He watched Sydney. She was talking softly to April, her voice soothing and patient.

"I guess she likes rocking like that," he said.

Sydney nodded. "It always worked for Lacey—my daughter. I just love little girls at this age. They're so sweet and innocent, then they get older and start piercing things and dyeing their hair."

"I saw her this morning. She's...colorful."

"And she came home with her eyebrow pierced last night. I just know the navel is next. When there's nothing left to pierce I'm sure she'll move on to tattoos."

He hoped he found April's family before he had to deal with anything like that. "You said you're a teacher. What grade?"

"Preschool."

"Sounds...demanding."

"It can be, but I love it. I couldn't imagine doing anything else."

"Where do you teach?"

Her smile wavered. "I'm sort of between jobs at the moment."

He wondered if she might be interested in babysitting for him until she found a new job. But as quickly as the idea formed, he dismissed it. Why would a teacher settle for a temporary babysitting gig? He could never match her salary.

April tensed suddenly, bucked in Sydney's lap and erupted like a volcano, spewing partially digested baby formula across the room. Daniel jumped out of the way but he was too slow. "Holy crap!"

"Projectile spit-up," Sydney said.

"I've never seen her do that before." He grabbed a burp cloth from the back of the couch and wiped curdled formula off his pant leg. "That must have been one heck of a gas bubble."

Daniel got on his hands and knees and cleaned up the mess. April was limp in Sydney's arms, her eyelids drooping. "She looks tired."

Sydney stood and gently raised April onto her shoulder. "Would you like me to lay her down in her crib?"

"That would be great."

Sydney carried April into the bedroom and placed her in the crib on her side, propping a blanket behind her back to hold her in place. April stirred for a moment, then curled her fist to her mouth and suckled in her sleep.

"I've never put her on her side before," Daniel whispered. "Will she sleep better?"

"Mine did. When she starts rolling over by herself you can put her on her stomach."

They stood together in silence, watching April sleep. Just an inch to the right and their forearms would touch, and for some reason the idea excited him. He glanced over at Sydney and she smiled, gazing up at him through a fringe of thick dark lashes. He hadn't noticed before, but her eyes were the same shade of blue as April's.

Maybe it was a sign.

It was a sign, all right. A sign that he needed to stay as far from this woman as humanly possible. Yes, she was hot, but she also had a kid, and she was the ex-wife of the most powerful man in town. He wasn't intimidated by the mayor and his lynch gang, but why invite drama to his life?

He gestured to the door and she followed him out into the hallway. "Thanks for your help."

"No problem. I take you don't have much experience with babies."

They walked to the living room. "Is my incompetence that obvious?"

She smiled, and it was somehow sweet and sexy at the same time. "You're babysitting?"

"Sort of. But there's a chance she could be with me awhile."

"Days?"

"Or months. It's tough to say at this point."

"Oh," she said, looking puzzled. "She's yours?"

"Not exactly. It's…complicated."

He could see that she was curious to know more, but to her credit, she didn't ask.

"I don't suppose you could recommend a babysitter?" he asked. "If I don't get back to work soon, I'm going to be out of a job."

She shook her head. "I haven't needed one in years." There was brief moment of awkward silence, then Sydney said, "Well, I should get home."

"Thanks again for your help. And for the casserole." He walked her to the door and pulled it open. "I'll bring your dish back later."

"No rush, and if April gives you any more trouble, just holler. I'll be home all day." She edged toward the door, glancing down the hall. "You could burp her in the middle of her feeding. That might settle her stomach and cut down on gas."

"I'll try that."

She took one step over the threshold. "And you could try soy formula. Some babies develop allergies to the regular kind. That could be why she's getting an upset tummy."

"Thanks, I'll remember that."

"Or you could—" She stopped, smiling sheepishly. "I'm sorry. You'll be fine. I'll see you later."

"Thanks, neighbor." He closed the door behind her and watched through the front window as she made her way across the lawn, her behind swaying beneath snug denim. And that hair. What was it about redheads that made him want to growl?

Abruptly, he turned away. No more leering at her, especially if he planned to talk her into working for him. Which he was seriously considering now, he realized. Temporarily, of course, until he found someone else and she found a job. He'd seen that sappy, lovesick look in her eyes when she'd held April. And he'd recognized her hesitancy before she left, as if he was totally unqualified to be alone with an infant. Which, let's face it, he probably was.

And his incompetence might be just the thing that would get her eating out of the palm of his hand.

As she unloaded groceries from the van later that afternoon, Sydney glanced next door, wondering how Deputy Valenzia was doing with April. She was dying to know why he would be taking care of a baby that wasn't his. Men with his reputation didn't make it a habit of taking in stray infants. Especially if it might cost him his job.

She heard the roar of a car engine coming down the street and turned to see Shane's car pull up in front of the house. The engine rumbled and the bass from the stereo reverberated through the pavement beneath her feet.

No wonder Lacey never seemed to hear her; the kid was probably deaf.

Sydney wasn't crazy about Lacey dating someone several years older, but Shane seemed like a decent kid and he came from a good family. Besides, forbidding Lacey to see Shane—as Jeff had wanted to do—would only make him that much more appealing. Having had a thing for bad boys when she was younger, Sydney knew this for a fact. It was how she'd ended up in Northern California in the first place. She'd followed her boyfriend—for which her mother had never forgiven her. And as her mom had predicted, the relationship hadn't lasted.

But then Jeff had taken an interest in her. Fifteen years her senior, he was rich, sophisticated and powerful. And worse for her than any "bad boy" she could have ever chosen.

How was that for irony?

Lacey ambled up the driveway, her usual obstinate self. "I'm home on time today. Are you happy?"

"Good. You can help with these." She thrust the heaviest bag in her daughter's arms, listening with

morbid satisfaction to her grumble all the way inside.
Sydney grabbed the last two bags and was walking to
the side door when she heard a bloodcurdling scream.
She charged inside and nearly collided head-on with
Fred McWilliams, Jeff's handyman.

"You scared me, Fred!" Sydney dropped the bags on
the kitchen table. "What are you doing here?"

Lacey glared at him, her eyes reduced to slits. "I
was putting away the groceries and he snuck up behind
me."

He smiled sheepishly. "Sorry, ma'am, I didn't mean
to scare her. Mr. Harris asked me to come by and see
about the air conditioner."

Sydney held back her anger. Wasn't it just like Jeff
to send someone out without warning her first? And
she didn't appreciate him giving people her key. Well,
it wasn't Fred's fault.

"I know Mr. Harris probably told you to come right
in, but I'd like my key back."

"Sure, Mrs. Harris." With his bony shoulders stooped,
he lumbered down the basement stairs.

"That guy gives me the creeps," Lacey said after his
footsteps faded.

"He'll be gone soon," Sydney assured her.

"He's a weirdo."

"No, he's just a little slow."

Sydney was sure he was harmless, but deep down
he gave her the creeps, too. The way he stared blankly
from under his greasy brown hair with beady eyes.
He had deep acne scars, and always reeked of strong
body odor.

"By the way," Lacey said. "Did you know we have a *cop* living next door?"

"I know. I met him yesterday. He seems…nice."

Lacey raised her slightly swollen brow.

"Not all police are bad, honey."

"How do you know he doesn't work for Dad, and he moved in next door to spy on us?"

Because your father doesn't care enough to take the trouble, she wanted to say, but held her tongue. "He seems okay."

"Veronica thinks he's hot."

Veronica would be correct.

"For an old guy," she added.

He couldn't be more than forty, though she was guessing closer to thirty-five. Sydney's age. "Old?"

Lacey rolled her eyes. "You know what I mean." She rummaged through one of the grocery bags and pulled out a bag of corn chips. "What's for dinner?"

"Chicken casserole, and don't even think about ruining your appetite with those chips."

"Fine." Lacey dropped the bag on the table. "I'm gonna work on my tan."

Sydney put away the groceries and popped the casserole into the oven. Gathering the ingredients for a salad, she chopped lettuce, tomatoes and carrots, dumping them all in a bowl. Turning to get the salad dressing from the fridge, she nearly plowed into Fred. She let out a startled squeak.

How long had he been standing there? "I didn't hear you come up the stairs, Fred. What do you want?"

"Sorry, ma'am." He sniffed loudly and wiped his nose with the back of his hand. "I'm finished."

"Fine."

"You want that fixed, too?" He gestured to the hole in the wall she hadn't yet gotten around to repatching.

"No, thanks, I'll take care of that myself."

He didn't move.

"Is there anything else?"

His bushy dark brows knit together. "Mr. Harris said you'd pay me."

"Oh, did he?" Bastard. She folded her arms over her chest. "Well, you tell Mr. Harris it's not my responsibility."

He still didn't budge, so she walked over to the side door and opened it. "Goodbye, Fred."

He sidled through, but she didn't miss the look of contempt he shot her as he passed. Tough. Jeff knew darn well the maintenance on the house was his responsibility.

Flinging the door shut, Sydney turned to the fridge for a bottle of Italian dressing and grabbed the cucumber she found hidden behind the mayonnaise jar. She put the dressing on the counter and dropped the cuke on the cutting board.

As she assembled the salad, she glanced out the window to the backyard. Lacey was in her bikini, sunning herself on a lounge chair, headphones on, her head swaying to the music. Sydney couldn't remember ever feeling so carefree as a teenager.

When she was thirteen, her dad bailed on them after years of dealing with her mom's chronic bouts of depression. Her mom had been so devastated by his leaving that for months she had barely been able to function. It had been up to Sydney to take care of her. But when her mother still refused to get help after a couple of years, Sydney had started to rebel. Deep down, she thought she could shake some sense into her mother.

She started small. Things like staying out past her curfew, and hanging out with boys who were much older. When that didn't work, she graduated to smoking and causing trouble at school. She lost track of how many times she'd been suspended. Then, when she was seventeen, she'd been hauled in for underage drinking and possession of marijuana. When her mom didn't show up to bail her out, it was the last straw.

Her boyfriend at the time, a twenty-two-year-old with zero potential, had been talking for months about moving to California, and for her it was the ultimate rebellion. So, off she went. Their relationship lasted six months, but by then Sydney was eighteen and had a decent job working as a server in a local pub. That was where she met Jeff. He'd showered her with affection and attention—the two things she had always craved from her mother but had never received—and treated her like a princess. By the time she realized that he was arrogant, dishonest and overbearing, she was pregnant with Lacey and felt she had to marry him.

She stayed with him for their daughter's sake, despite his many affairs. But clearly that had done more harm than good. For her and Lacey.

Sometimes when she looked at Lacey, it was like looking in the mirror. Which was why she tried so hard to shelter her from the worst of it. She needed time to just…be a kid.

Lacey was now drumming her knees to the beat of the music and lip-syncing the words. Sydney smiled. Everything she'd worked for, the peace she fought for, was all for Lacey.

Sydney set the table and, as an afterthought, chopped an onion to go with the salad.

"Dinner ready?" Lacey asked from behind her, and Sydney jumped a mile, nearly chopping off a few fingers in the process.

"Please stop sneaking up on me," she said, glancing at her daughter, discreetly checking her bikini-clad body for new holes.

"Fred just left." Lacey plucked a cherry tomato from the bowl and popped it in her mouth. "He was watching me."

Sydney's brow furrowed. Hadn't Fred left a while ago? "What do you mean, watching you?"

"I mean, I opened my eyes and he was standing by the side of the house looking at me, then he walked away. He's a total creep."

"You know, I'm beginning to agree with you, Lacey. If you see him again, you let me know, and keep your distance."

"Like I'd want to be anywhere near him," she scoffed. "He's gross. When's dinner?"

"Ten minutes. I'll call you when it's ready."

Sydney finished dinner, keeping an eye out the kitchen window in case Fred returned. He had no business staring at Lacey. The idea made her uneasy. Maybe he wasn't as harmless as they had thought…and he'd forgotten to give her key back. Or maybe he hadn't forgotten. Maybe he'd kept it on purpose. And now he could get in whenever he felt like it.

First thing in the morning, she would call a locksmith and have every lock in the house changed. If Fred had the gall to stand there and leer at Lacey in broad daylight, who knew what he was capable of in the privacy of a house.

Later that evening, when Lacey went out to a movie with Shane, Sydney stood on the porch until the car was out of sight, and couldn't shake the feeling she was being watched.

You're imagining things, she assured herself. But as the sun began to set, casting long, eerie shadows, she began to think that waiting until morning to change the locks had been a bad idea. She pulled out the phone book, but every place that she called was either closed or couldn't come until the morning. She made an appointment for 9:00 a.m. then turned on every light in the house and locked all of the windows. She even hooked a chair under the doorknob in the living room—just in case.

God help me if there's a fire, she thought, hitching a second chair under the knob of the side door. She would just have to sit up and wait for Lacey, so she could let her in the house.

She jumped when the phone rang.

"My secretary told me you called," Jeff said, sounding annoyed.

"Fred came by today. I don't ever want to see him here again."

"Jesus, what's your problem now?"

"He scares Lacey."

"So?"

"What do you mean, *so?* She was lying out in a bikini and she said he was watching her. It makes her uncomfortable and it worries me. What do you really know about him?"

"He's a good handyman and he's cheap. If you don't like it, pay for the damned repairs yourself."

"You're willing to put our daughter's peace of mind, not to mention her safety, at risk to save a few dollars?"

"Lacey would say anything for attention. Get a clue."

Get a clue? Was he kidding? He was the clueless one.

"I'm tired of you using Lacey to manipulate me. Keep it up and I'll have to sic my lawyer on you. You're warping our daughter and I won't let you get away with it."

She heard a loud click and the phone went dead. "You stupid jerk."

She slammed the phone down and paced the kitchen floor, hating Jeff more than she'd ever hated another human being. And calling Jeff a human being was a serious stretch in itself. He was lower than human, lower than—

A flash of movement in her peripheral vision caught her attention and she spun toward the side door. She froze, her heart battering her rib cage. The curtains were open a fraction of an inch and she saw a glimmer of color under the side porch light.

Someone was outside.

Would Fred have the nerve to come right up to a lit doorway and force his way in? He couldn't be that demented. She slowly leaned forward, craning her neck to peek past the curtains, and nearly jumped out of her skin at the loud rap.

CHAPTER FOUR

IT WASN'T FUNNY, not at all, but Daniel couldn't seem to wipe the grin off of his face. Especially now that the color had returned to Sydney's face and her eyes had gone back to their normal size.

"I really am sorry," he said again. "I didn't mean to scare you. When I saw all of your lights on, I thought you wouldn't mind me stopping by."

"You don't have to apologize. I've been a little edgy today, that's all."

She tried to smile, but it didn't quite reach her eyes. Her mouth looked great anyway—lush and pink, full and pouty. And he reminded himself once again not to look at it. He had a job to do here, so to speak.

April fussed, so he readjusted her in his lap, and she lunged for the plastic key ring he'd placed just out of reach on the edge of the kitchen table. He'd discovered if she thought she wasn't supposed to have something, it made it that much more fun to play with.

Sydney reached for the baby and April squealed, her arms shooting forth at the invitation. *Good girl,* Daniel thought. She was making his job a lot easier.

"So, what's with the chair in front of the door?" he asked, nodding toward the living room. "I'm sure I don't have to tell you how unsafe that is."

"I got spooked. We had a sort of...incident today."

He frowned, wondering what her ex had done this time. Because he didn't doubt for a second that whatever it was, the mayor was probably responsible. "What sort of incident?"

She told him about the handyman, and the mayor's total lack of regard for his daughter's safety. Daniel wasn't surprised. In his line of work, he'd seen ex-husbands and wives do a lot worse to each other.

"What did you say the guy's name is?" he asked, pulling out his cell phone.

"Fred McWilliams."

"Age?"

She shrugged. "Mid-twenties, maybe."

He dialed the sheriff's office and Margie answered.

"Sheriff Montgomery's not in," she told him.

"I called to talk to you. I need a favor. Could you run a name for me?"

"Sure, honey. What is it?"

He gave her the information, and the McWilliams guy was in the system.

"He was collared last year for a drunk and disorderly, and he's got a DUI from three years ago. You want me to dig deeper?"

"Nope, that was all I needed. Thanks." He disconnected. "I don't think you have anything to worry about, Sydney. His only vice seems to be a tendency to drink, but he's never hurt anyone."

Sydney looked relieved. "I still wish the locksmith could have come tonight, but I'm not as worried."

"A trick I learned, if you can put a drop of super glue

in the key hole, it's impossible to get a key in. But only do it if you're sure the locksmith is coming, or you won't be able to leave the house."

"Thanks, Daniel. I really appreciate your help." April let out an earsplitting squeal and Sydney sat her on the table top in front of her. "So, what's the problem with you tonight, little girl?"

Daniel gave Sydney the baffled I'm-an-incompetent-moron look he'd been practicing. "She just won't go to sleep. I even started her on that formula you suggested."

"Is that true?" Sydney cooed, standing April in her lap. April screeched and bounced up and down on her chubby little legs.

"She sure does like you," he said.

"We girls have to stick together, don't we, April?" April let out another high-pitched squeal and latched on to a lock of Sydney's hair with a sticky fist. Sydney laughed and tugged it loose. "Did she sleep much for you today?"

"Most of the afternoon, but tonight she just fussed when I put her to bed." Actually, he hadn't tried all that hard to get her to sleep, but Sydney didn't have to know that part. She just had to think he didn't know what he was doing, which he didn't.

"You wouldn't want to go to bed at night, either, if you slept all day." She nuzzled April's nose with her own and the baby gurgled.

"I guess not." He just frowned and tried to look confused, scratching the stubble on his chin.

"Growing a beard?" she asked, glancing in his direction.

"Me?" He rubbed his rough cheek. "Nah, I just didn't feel like shaving today."

"Today?"

"Okay," he conceded. "This week."

"You might want to consider it."

"Growing a beard?"

"No, *shaving.*"

He sat back and folded his arms across his chest. "Why? You don't like hairy men?"

He could swear she blushed a little.

"I was thinking it probably feels like steel wool against April's skin." She tickled April's chin. "What do you think, honey? Does he need to shave off those icky whiskers?"

"You know, I never even thought of that." She did get really squirmy when he held her sometimes. Maybe he was hurting her and didn't know it. This parenting gig could be really complicated.

"Any luck finding a nanny today?" she asked.

He sat a bit straighter in his chair. "Why? Are you interested?"

She blinked rapidly. "N-no, of course not, I just...I was only curious."

Did she think he was angry that she'd asked? She was a tough one to figure out. One minute she was completely at ease, then bam, she wouldn't even look him in the eye. Maybe it was the badge, and her previous run-ins with the mayor's posse. Maybe she thought he was on her ex's payroll.

If he had any hope of persuading her to work for him, he was going to have to set the record straight.

"I make you nervous." he said.

"Why would you think that?" she asked, but she wouldn't meet his eye.

"Just a hunch. And considering your recent experiences with the local law, I can't say I blame you. But let me make myself clear. I think your ex is an ass."

She finally looked at him, but her eyes were wary. "I'd like to believe that."

He couldn't blame her for her apprehension. Which made the idea of tricking her into wanting to work for him feel downright sleazy.

"The truth is, I didn't come over here because I needed help with April. I just wanted you to think I was incompetent, so you might take pity on me and agree to be my nanny."

Her eyes widened. "You want *me* to be your nanny?"

"Only temporarily. I thought, since you're between jobs, it would be the ideal situation for us both. Until I either find someone permanent, or I locate April's family."

"Deputy Valenzia—"

"Daniel."

"*Daniel,* I'm sure you've heard the rumors—"

"I told you, your ex is an ass. I'm not inclined to believe anything he says."

"I appreciate that you trust me, but hiring me is tantamount to painting a target on your back."

"The mayor doesn't scare me. And like I said before,

if I don't find someone soon, I'm going to be out of a job. I'm desperate, Sydney."

She frowned, looking conflicted. "I don't know..."

"Don't make me beg."

"Can you give me a night to think about it?"

He nearly sighed with relief. That was a start. "Of course."

April pulled at the buttons on Sydney's shirt and let out a wail of frustration when they wouldn't come loose. Sydney cradled her against her chest, but she still squirmed and fussed. "I think she's getting tired."

"I should try feeding her and putting her down again." He stood and reached for April. "Thanks for your help."

"I didn't do much."

He glanced over at the chair in front of the door. "Have you got a pen and paper?"

"Sure." She got them from a kitchen drawer.

He wrote down his cell number. "Here's my number. If you get scared for any reason or just need to hear a friendly voice, give me a call. I'm usually up well past midnight."

She smiled. "Thank you."

"Don't hesitate to call. Anytime."

She walked him to the side door and pulled it open. "Good luck with April tonight."

"Thanks. And you try not to worry, okay? I'm right next door if you need me." He paused at the door and added, "I'll talk to you tomorrow?"

She nodded and smiled, and he had the strangest urge to lean in and press his lips to hers. Or maybe it wasn't strange. Maybe the fact that she was so different from the type of woman he was normally attracted to was what intrigued him. Or maybe it was just that she was attractive and available, and he'd been in a month-long dry spell. Maybe if the circumstances were different, he might indulge in a short fling.

But if Sydney did agree to work for him, she was off limits.

DANIEL ROLLED ONTO HIS BACK and stretched, slowly waking from the deepest sleep he'd had in weeks. The steady drum of a spring rain beating against the window registered through a groggy haze. Opening his eyes, he shifted up onto his elbow to read the display on the digital clock on the night table.

Eight forty-five.

Eight forty-five? He shot straight up in bed. He'd put April to bed at midnight. She should have been awake hours ago!

Frantically he kicked off the blankets. Something was wrong. She'd never slept more than a three- or four-hour stretch at night. A million different horrific images shot through his brain. He ran for the door, tripping over his tennis shoes and tumbling into the hall. He skidded to a stop outside April's door, fear growing in the pit of his stomach.

What would he find on the other side?

Poised with his hand on the knob, heart lodged in his throat, he heard a noise. A soft, playful babbling. A surge of relief coursed through him, and his legs threatened to buckle.

As quietly as he could manage, he eased the door open a crack, peeking into the dim room. April had rolled from her side to her stomach and turned one hundred and eighty degrees, scooting herself to the foot of the crib, grasping at the bumper pads, speaking in baby talk to the colorful images of farm animals. He wrestled with the urge to scoop her up out of the crib and hug her. She seemed so content playing, he hated to disturb her.

A grin spread across his face. She was a cute little runt, despite all the trouble she'd caused. And he felt guilty that he couldn't keep her, couldn't honor Reanne's wishes. The best he could do was find her real family. She would be better off with them.

The low rumble of thunder made the window above the crib vibrate and a brilliant flash of lightning lit the room. April turned her head and blinked several times—not frightened, just inquisitive—then she saw Daniel leaning in the doorway and squealed, kicking her little legs.

"G'morning, munchkin." He crossed the room and picked her up, lifting her high over his head until she giggled excitedly, then he drew her into his arms and hugged her tight. She was so soft and warm, so sweet. He'd always loved kids. He'd even been something of a surrogate father to his nephew, but never before had he felt this urge to nurture and protect.

"You scared Uncle Danny half to death," he told her. Uncle Danny. Somehow that just didn't sound right, but neither did plain old Danny or Daniel. *Daddy* definitely wasn't right, either. He hated to slap a label on their situation when he wasn't sure how long she would be around. He'd called Joe yesterday to check if there were any leads in finding April's family, but so far nothing. If her real father wanted her, assuming he even knew she existed, wouldn't he have come forward by now?

All Daniel could do for now was just wait and see.

SHE WAS GOING to do it.

It had taken her one long, sleepless night to make the decision, but now Sydney was sure. She was going to be April's nanny.

Temporarily.

Deputy Val—*Daniel*—needed her help. And now that she was out of a job, what else would she do with her time? She could overlook the fact that he was a cop because he hated Jeff and his cronies, and the fact that he trusted her despite the rumors earned him some pretty major brownie points. His sizzling good looks…okay, those might be a little harder to overlook. But knowing his reputation, he would never be interested in a woman with so much baggage anyway.

"It's the right thing to do," she rationalized.

She looked out the kitchen window and saw that his truck was in the driveway. The earlier heavy rain had eased off but it was still the kind of dreary, depressing drizzle that would likely last all day.

What the heck, it was only a couple hundred feet to his porch. A little rain wouldn't kill her. Opening the side door, she started out. She'd made it to the edge of her property when a bolt of lightning zigzagged across the sky and a simultaneous crack of thunder shook the ground beneath her feet. The sky opened up again and icy rain came down in a torrent. She ran the rest of the way to Daniel's porch, drenched to the skin by the time she made it under the overhang. She banged on his door and it swung open almost immediately.

"Jeez, what happened to you?" Daniel said, looking her over from head to toe.

"Can I come in?" she asked. "Before I drown?"

He held the door open, looking out. "It's really pouring out there."

"You think?" The minute she crossed the threshold into the air-conditioned room, she started to shiver.

"You don't have an umbrella?"

"When I left the house it was only sprinkling." She tried to rub warmth into her sodden arms. "Do you maybe have a towel I could use?"

"Of course, sorry."

He dashed to the kitchen, and while she waited a noise behind the sofa caught her attention. She craned her neck to see over the back where April lay in a play-pen, swinging her hands at the play set hanging over her head. She batted a black-and-white-striped triangle and gurgled happily.

What was it about babies that made Sydney feel all mushy inside? Though it didn't used to be that way. She had always sworn she would never have kids. And after she got pregnant with Lacey, at first, she had been devastated. But the first time she heard Lacey's heartbeat in the doctor's office, she fell hopelessly in love.

Even though she was dripping on Daniel's floor,

Sydney tiptoed around the couch and peeked into the playpen.

April saw her and broke into a wide smile.

"Hi, sweetheart. Are you playing?"

April kicked her legs and squealed.

Suddenly Sydney was enveloped in something soft and warm.

"I had a load finishing up in the dryer," Daniel said, tucking the thick bath towel around her shoulders from behind. "It should warm you up." He dropped a smaller towel on the floor to soak up the puddle she'd made. "Take off your shoes."

She slipped out of them and stepped on to the towel. She should have stayed by the door. "Sorry about your floor."

Taking her by the shoulders and turning her to face him, he rubbed her arms through the towel. He still hadn't shaved, and his stubble was becoming a full-blown beard. "I don't care about the floor. I just didn't want you to slip and break your neck. I found out the hard way how slippery this hardwood can be. I was walking from the shower to the laundry room this morning and my feet flew right out from under me." He grimaced and rubbed his backside. "I'm still not sitting quite right."

She envisioned him with only a towel loosely fastened about his waist, his olive skin glistening and dewy.

Oh, boy. Definitely not the kind of thoughts she should be having. And that would be much easier if he stopped standing so close. And stopped *touching* her.

He stepped back and gestured to the couch. "Sit down."

She did, and he sat on the chair across from her. "So, did you get your locks changed this morning?"

"I did. I hardly slept at all last night. I was afraid that if I tried your glue trick something would happen and the locksmith wouldn't be able to make it for days."

"Tell me you at least moved the chair."

She looked down at her hands.

"Should I tell you about the bodies I've seen pulled out of burning buildings—"

"Ew, no! Please don't. I won't do it again."

There was genuine concern in his eyes. "I'll hold you to that."

She wondered what he would think of the chair she'd hooked under the side door, but figured it wasn't worth mentioning. "So, I've given your offer a lot of thought."

"And?" he said, looking anxious.

"And I'll do it."

He slumped with relief. "Thank God."

"However," she added, "I need to know what the situation is. Whose baby she is. If some woman shows up at the door saying April is hers, I need to know what to do."

"April's mother won't be showing up. She's dead."

CHAPTER FIVE

SYDNEY SUCKED IN a quiet breath. "How did she die?"

"Cancer," Daniel told her. "According to the social worker, she was diagnosed when she was pregnant. And knowing it could hurt the baby, she refused treatment until after April was born. But by then, I guess, it was too late."

"That's so sad. You were good friends with her?"

"That's the really strange thing. I hardly knew her. We had a brief affair. She wasn't in town long enough for me to get to know her very well. She was something of a drifter. No permanent home. She told me she grew up in the foster care system, so she probably didn't want April to end up there. I guess that's why she put my name on the birth certificate."

"You're sure you're not her father?"

"Not unless Reanne was pregnant for fifteen months."

"You mentioned trying to find April's family."

"I figure there has to be someone. At least, I'm hoping there is."

"You don't want to keep her?"

"What do I know about raising kids? I never even planned to have any." After watching his parents' marriage crash and burn, and seeing the way it affected his sisters, he'd decided never to marry. Sure, it could get lonely at times, but living in a tourist town, he never ran out of available women to date.

"It would be a huge responsibility for a single guy," she said.

"I don't exactly lead a lifestyle conducive to raising a kid. I'm a cop. Even though we don't get a lot of violent crimes in Prospect, it's still a dangerous line of work. If I were killed, what would happen to April then?"

"Foster care," Sydney said.

"Exactly. Which I'm assuming is what Reanne didn't want."

"Have you considered adoption?"

"If I can't find her biological family, that will be my only other option." Sydney looked troubled, so he asked, "You think I'm a bad person for giving her up?"

Her expression softened. "No, of course not. I was just thinking how tough it will be for her at first, being bounced around. But kids are resilient. And it's obvious you've taken good care of her. I take you didn't already have the baby furniture and toys and bottles. Or the house."

"I got most of it at second-hand shops. And I had been planning to move into a bigger place eventually, anyway. The one-room loft wasn't cutting it anymore. This just sped things up a bit."

"I'd say you've gone above the call of duty. She's lucky to have you."

"Well, I haven't done it all on my own. The first few weeks, my sisters helped a lot."

"How many do you have?"

"Five."

Sydney's eyes went wide. "*Five?* Wow. Older or younger?"

"Angie—Angelica—is my twin, and the other four—Abigail, Bethany, Delilah and Leah—are younger."

"That's a big family."

"Yeah, considering my parents never should have gotten married in the first place. I'm sure there must have been a time when they loved each other, but I never saw it."

"Divorced?"

"When I was seventeen."

"I was thirteen when my dad bailed on me and my mom."

"You're an only child?" he asked.

"I had a brother. He was four years younger than me, but he died when he was three months old from SIDS. My mom never really recovered. She was severely depressed for years. Still is, as far as I know. I think she blamed herself for his death."

April let out a warning shriek, one that usually meant she was about to start wailing. Daniel walked to the playpen and picked her up. Her diaper was wet. "I have to change her."

Sydney shot up from her seat. "Do you want me to do it?"

"I've got it. But why don't you come with me and I can show you where everything is."

"Sure," she said, following him to April's room.

While he wrestled April into a new diaper he gave

Sydney a quick rundown of where she could find things.

"Maybe I can help you organize," she said, eyeing the moving clutter that he hadn't yet found a place for.

"That would be a big help." He lifted April off the changing table and turned to Sydney. She stood in the doorway, the towel still draped over her shoulders, and... *hello*.

She must have been chilled, because he could see the outline of her nipples through her damp shirt. It was as if they were calling to him, silently begging him to notice.

He noticed. And God help him, he appreciated the view. His first thought was to ask if she'd ever been in a wet T-shirt contest. A clear indication that a month without female companionship was taking its toll. Maybe he could talk one of his sisters into watching April next Friday evening so he could go out. An evening at Moose Winooski's, the local brewery, was exactly what he needed to shake off the stress of a month in captivity.

With any luck, the P.I. would find someone to take April soon, and Daniel would have his life back.

He realized that he'd zoned out staring at Sydney's chest, and she must have noticed, too, because she pulled the towel down to cover herself.

"Did you want to hold her?" he asked.

She looked longingly at April, but said, "I shouldn't while I'm all wet."

"Maybe we should talk about money," he said.

"Money?" she asked, confused.

"I do plan to pay you to watch April."

"Oh, right. Sure."

"Let's go back to the family room." He carried April over to the playpen and laid her inside, hoping she would play a little while longer before lunch. Sydney sat on the couch, and he took a seat beside her. Maybe it was his imagination, but she seemed uneasy. Maybe she just didn't like talking finances.

"I'm not sure what the going rate for a nanny is, and I doubt I can even come close to matching your former salary—"

"Why don't you just pay me what you can afford?"

What if what he could afford was less than what she needed? Or maybe whatever he could pay was better than no pay at all. "I want to be fair. Why don't you give me a number. What you would expect for, say, a forty-hour week."

She though about it for a minute, then quoted a sum that even he considered ridiculously low. Not that he wouldn't love a great deal, but it wouldn't be right to take advantage of her. "Are you sure that's enough?"

"Let's just say that I'm not hurting for money."

He recalled hearing a rumor that she'd taken her ex to the cleaners in the divorce. It appeared as though it wasn't just a rumor after all.

"Besides," she added. "Think how convenient this will be for me. No morning commute, and if I have things to do at home, I can just bring her with me."

"True," he said, but it still seemed low to him. "You should know that occasionally I work the night shift."

"I don't have a problem with that. And maybe if I get a parking ticket…"

He grinned. "It would be nice if it disappeared?"

"Not that I would ever ask you to do anything unethical."

"You get a lot of tickets?"

"Over eight hundred dollars' worth in the past year."

He winced. That was blatant harassment. He didn't doubt the mayor's posse was responsible. And though fixing it for her could put him in hot water, it would be worth a minor scalding or two. "Consider it done."

"When do you need me to start?"

"Is Monday too soon?"

"Monday is fine." She paused and then asked, "So we have a deal?"

If she wanted to work for peanuts, who was he to tell her no? "Yeah, we have a deal."

He extended a hand to shake on it, and she hesitated before she slid her hand into his.

It was ice-cold. "Sydney, you're freezing," he said, rubbing her hand between both of his to warm it. "Why didn't you say something? I could have loaned you a sweatshirt."

She extracted her hand from his grasp and wound it with its mate in her lap, eyes lowered. "I-I'm fine."

There she went again, getting all nervous. Maybe it would just take time for her to trust him.

But what if it had nothing to do with the fact that he was law enforcement? What if she was nervous because she was attracted to him? Now that he considered it, she seemed to get edgy whenever he got close or touched her.

Testing the theory, he leaned casually against the cushion and rested his arm on the back of the couch behind her head. She tensed, and he smothered a wry smile.

Maybe she *was* attracted to him. Either that or she was uncomfortable with men in general. Or maybe she hadn't been with one in a while. Far as he could recall, she'd split with her ex at least a year ago, and he'd never seen her at any of the local singles hot spots since then. And since he'd moved in next door he hadn't noticed any men—besides her sleazebag ex—dropping by.

"Do your sisters live in Prospect?" she asked. Nervously, as though she felt the need to fill the silence.

He turned slightly, so that his knee was barely an inch from her thigh. "Angie, Beth and Dee live here. Abbi lives in Colorado and Leah is going to school in New York."

"And your parents?"

"My dad passed away three years ago. My mom lives in town. She works at the resort as an activities director."

He reached out and wound a damp ringlet of Sydney's hair around his index finger. "Would you like a towel for your hair?"

"No." She eased away from him, awkwardly smoothing her hair back down and tucking the ringlet behind her ear. "Thanks."

"Something wrong?" he asked.

"O-of course not."

"Are you sure? You seem awfully nervous."

"I'm fine."

"Are you?" He shifted so that his knee brushed her bare thigh and she jumped. "Call me crazy, Sydney, but I get the suspicion that you might be attracted to me."

SYDNEY BLINKED in rapid succession. "E-excuse me?"

"You're acting like you might be attracted to me," Daniel said again, even though she'd heard him perfectly fine the first time. "Are you?"

"What kind of question is that?" And why was he asking? And why were her cheeks suddenly on fire with embarrassment?

He couldn't actually be trying to seduce her, could he? Did he think that was part of the babysitting package? She had to admit, it would be one hell of a perk, but even if she was in the market for a fling, it would never be with a man like him. He was way out of her league. He oozed sex appeal, and for years Jeff had referred to her as the Ice Queen.

"I'm wondering if that's why you're so nervous around me."

"I just don't like cops."

"But you *know* I'm a good cop. If you didn't, you never would have agreed to watch April. And you only get nervous when I get close, or do something like this." His fingers brushed her earlobe.

"Stop that!" she said, batting his hand away.

He grinned, and if it hadn't been so damned adorable she probably would have decked him.

"I rest my case," he said, looking pleased with himself.

She hated that she was so skittish around men. It had just been so long since one had noticed her. And even longer since one had touched her. Not that she'd put herself in the position to be the object of anyone's interest. The one time she'd let her hair down and had fun, she'd been hauled off in handcuffs. Staying home just seemed safer.

"Even if I was attracted to you," she said, "I would *never* date a cop. Or someone I worked for. Or *anyone* nicknamed Deputy Casanova."

"And I would never date a single mom," he said. "Or a next-door neighbor."

Yet his impish grin said dating her was irrelevant, and he had something else entirely in mind.

Freedom.

Daniel watched as his mom backed out of the driveway and drove off, April strapped securely in the backseat. She had agreed to watch April not just for the evening, but overnight, and it was a night he didn't intend to spend alone.

He took the longest shower he'd had in a month, then shaved. He dressed in jeans, cowboy boots and a black PCSD—Prospect County Sheriff Department—T-shirt. He grabbed his keys from the kitchen counter and was heading out the side door when he noticed Sydney's dish sitting there. He'd forgotten to give it to her yesterday when she came by. And remembering her visit, the way she had jumped when he touched her, made him grin. She'd more or less admitted she was attracted to him. But, attracted to each other or not, they seemed to have an understanding that a relationship would be a bad idea.

He grabbed the dish and crossed the yard to Sydney's side door. He knocked, and it swung open a few seconds later. But it wasn't Sydney, it was her daughter.

"Hi, I'm Daniel from next door. Is your mom home?"

"Mom!" she called over her shoulder and held the door so Daniel could step inside. "The cop from next door is here!"

She looked as though she was probably a cute kid under the dark makeup and green hair. She had Sydney's wide blue eyes and upturned nose.

"You must be Lacey," he said.

"My mom said you hired her to be your nanny."

He couldn't tell if she thought that was a good thing or a bad thing. "Are you okay with that?"

"Sure. Considering my tool of a father got her fired from her job."

He smothered a grin. Apparently Lacey's opinion of her father wasn't much better than Sydney's.

"Don't call your father a *tool,* sweetheart," Sydney said, appearing in the kitchen doorway.

"Well, he is one," Lacey mumbled, then a car horn blared outside. "That's Veronica. Gotta go!"

She slipped past Daniel and out the back door, and Sydney called after her, "Have fun, honey! See you tomorrow!"

"Cute kid," Daniel said.

"Who obviously has issues with her father."

"I guess you can't exactly blame her." He held out

the dish to her. "I forgot to give this back. The casserole was good. Maybe I can get the recipe?"

She took the dish, eyeing him suspiciously. "You cook?"

"I'm thirty-six and single. It was learn to cook or live on fast food and frozen dinners."

For the first time since Sydney had walked into the room, Daniel really focused on her face and realized her eyes were a little swollen and red-rimmed, as if she'd been crying. Had she had a run-in with her ex? He felt his hackles rise. "What's wrong?"

His concern seemed to confuse her. "Why would you think that?"

"You look like you've been crying. Did your ex do something?"

She laughed. "No, nothing like that. I was watching a movie on Lifetime. Friday is usually movie night for me."

"But it's a gorgeous evening. You should get out. Have fun."

"The last time I did that, I was arrested. I feel safer staying home."

"Don't you miss seeing your friends?"

She shifted uncomfortably. "The truth is, I don't really have any. Jeff got them in the divorce."

Then they were even stupider than the mayor. And it bugged Daniel that Sydney was afraid to go out and have fun. She deserved better than that.

Before he could think what he was doing, he said, "Go get dressed."

She looked down at her T-shirt and shorts. "I am dressed."

"I mean, get *dressed,* I'm taking you out."

Her eyes widened, and she shook her head. "I told you, I don't date cops."

"It's not a date. It's just friends going out for a drink. And you *need* to get out."

"No, I don't."

"Trust me, you do." He took her by the shoulders, turned her in the direction of the kitchen door, and gave her a gentle shove. "Now go. And wear something… sexy."

She shot him a look over her shoulder.

"Trust me."

She reluctantly left the room, then he heard her bedroom door close. The reason, he figured, for her tendency to be nervous around him, was a complete lack of self-confidence. Which was totally unwarranted because she was a beautiful woman. Not to mention really nice. And if she was ever going to get her confidence back, she had to put herself out there. He knew a dozen guys on the force who would trip over each other to dance with her. If not because she was hot as hell, then out of curiosity because she was the ex of the biggest ass in a thirty-mile radius.

He took a seat at her kitchen table and waited, looking at his watch occasionally, hoping Sydney wasn't one of those women who took hours to get ready. Fifteen minutes passed before she appeared in the doorway.

"I'm ready."

He looked up and gave a low whistle. "Wow."

She'd dressed in form-fitting jeans that hugged all the right places, spike-heeled boots and a scoop-neck, sleeveless blouse made of some silky, layered fabric so transparent he could just make out the silhouette of her bra underneath. And the cleavage spilling out over the top...

Damn.

She'd put her hair up, leaving a few curls loose to frame her face and brush her neck. She'd applied only a little mascara and shiny lip gloss, but honestly, she didn't need more than that. She looked...breathtaking.

"Too much?" she asked, shifting nervously.

"Perfect," he said. She was going to have to beat men off with a stick. He got to his feet. "You ready?"

"I'm still not sure about this."

"You'll have a great time. Trust me."

She looked as if she might argue, then she grabbed her purse off the kitchen counter and said, "Let's go before I change my mind."

They crossed the lawn to his truck, and he opened the door for her.

"Buckle up," he said, as he climbed in the driver's seat.

She fidgeted beside him, as though any second she might throw the door open, jump out and make a run for it.

"Relax," he told her. "You're going to have fun."

He started the truck, backed out of the driveway, and headed in the direction of town. Thankfully it was only a few minutes' drive, so she didn't have much time to change her mind.

As they turned onto Main Street traffic grew thicker. The sidewalks were congested with tourists and locals. Though daytime activities kept most of the visitors up at the resort, town nightlife drew them down the mountain to the main strip. And because there was an antique car show this weekend, the city was exceptionally busy.

"I forgot to ask where we're going," she said

"Moose Winooski's."

She was dead silent, so he looked over at her and realized that most of the color had leached from her face. "What's wrong?"

"Jeff hangs out there."

"Sometimes. So what?"

"You don't think that will be…awkward?"

Probably not for the mayor, who seemed to think he owned the town. Which was exactly why she needed to go. "If he's there, ignore him. If he hassles you, I'll take care of it."

"He's not someone you want to piss off, Daniel."

"I told you before, I'm not afraid of him."

The brewery parking lot was already filled to capacity but they found a spot on a side street a block down. After he parked, Sydney reached for the door handle. "Don't touch that," he told her.

She yanked her hand back. "Why?"

He got out and walked around the truck and tugged her door open. "Because you deserve to be treated like a lady."

For the first time that night, she smiled. But as they walked down the street toward the entrance, the smile turned into a grimace.

"Don't be nervous," Daniel said.

"I'm not nervous. I'm *terrified*."

Her steps slowed, and since he figured there was a good possibility she might turn tail and run, he grabbed her hand. As they neared the building, they could hear a cover of a Tim McGraw song blaring from within, played by the local country western band that performed every Friday and Saturday night.

When they got to the door he pulled it open and had to practically shove her through. The bar was packed, as was the dance floor, and every table seemed to be occupied.

"Danny!" someone shouted, and he craned his neck to see Jon Montgomery, one of his fellow deputies, waving him over to the bar. He stood with a group of Daniel's friends. Keeping a tight grip on Sydney's hand he dragged her along with him, letting go only to shake hands with Jon.

"Where the hell you been?" Jon asked, and when he saw Sydney standing there, it was as if Daniel ceased to exist. "And who is this lovely woman?"

"This is a friend of mine, Sydney Harris," Daniel said. "Sydney, this is Jon."

Jon took Sydney's hand, but instead of shaking it, he kissed it instead. "A pleasure to meet you, Sydney Harris."

She flashed him a wobbly smile. "Hi."

Daniel heard someone call his name and turned to see his twin sister coming toward them.

"Hey, Angie," he said and reached out to give her

a hug. But Angie ignored him and went straight for Sydney.

"You must be Sydney," she said, pumping Sydney's hand. "It's so good to finally meet you."

Sydney looked a little confused.

"Sydney, this is my sister Angie," Daniel said.

Angie laughed. "I guess I could have introduced myself, huh? You're probably thinking, who is this crazy woman accosting me?"

"No, I figured it out," Sydney told her. "You look a lot alike."

"We favor our father. He was born in Argentina. Our mother is pure Irish. And she's dying to meet you, by the way. Maybe we could do lunch some day? Just the three of us? Of course, Beth and Dee will probably want to come, too. They're our younger sisters."

"Um, sure," Sydney said, seeming uncertain. Daniel didn't blame her; Angie did have the tendency to come on a little strong.

"Danny tells me you have a fifteen-year-old daughter. I have a seventeen-year-old son." She turned to Daniel. "Speaking of kids, where's April?"

"Mom has her for the night."

"Oh! Well, maybe I'll stop over there tomorrow morning so I can see her."

"I'm going to introduce Sydney around," Daniel told his sister, before she really got going.

"Of course," Angie said, shooing them away. "We'll talk later."

Daniel took Sydney by the shoulders and maneuvered her to the opposite end of the bar, saying under his breath, "So, is your head spinning?"

"A little. But I liked her."

Daniel introduced Sydney to his friends and everyone seemed eager to meet the mayor's ex. She was a little reserved at first, staying glued to his side, but after a while she started to relax. Eventually one of the women dragged her off to chat with a group of wives and girl-friends. And after a beer or two, she actually started to look as though she was having fun.

"So, is she the Sydney Harris I think she is?" Daniel's friend Russ, the only trustworthy mechanic in town, asked. "The mayor's ex?"

"Yep." Daniel took a swallow of his beer, watching as one of the local firefighters asked Sydney to dance, and she reluctantly followed him out onto the dance floor.

David Smith, a fellow deputy who was leaning on the bar to Daniel's left, asked, "And she's just a friend?"

"Yep."

"*Why?* She's *hot.*" That earned him a slug from his wife, Sammi.

"Watch it, pal," she warned, but she was grinning. She and David had started dating in high school, married a week after graduation and had been going strong ever since. Daniel wished all marriages could be so stable, but he knew they were the exception to the rule.

"I'll admit it was tempting," Daniel said. "But she's my next-door neighbor, she has a kid, and starting Monday she's going to be April's nanny."

"You know how pissed Harris would be if his ex was

dating a cop," Jon said. "Especially one who refuses to play by his rules."

"Speak of the devil," Sammi said, nodding to the door. "Look who just walked in."

CHAPTER SIX

DANIEL TURNED to see Jeff Harris come in, his girl-friend clinging to his arm, a member of his posse on either side. He watched with morbid curiosity as the mayor did a quick scan of the bar, then the dance floor, knowing the exact second he spotted Sydney. His brow lifted in surprise, then instantly lowered.

Oh, yeah, he wasn't happy. That gave Daniel way more satisfaction than it should have.

Daniel looked over at Sydney, but she seemed oblivious to the fact that her ex was there. And he hoped it stayed that way. She was actually having fun now. He didn't want Harris to spoil it.

A rookie cop—who had to be at least ten years younger than Sydney, cut in and the firefighter walked off dejectedly.

"I get the feeling he would be pissed no matter who she was dating. He seems to get off on making her miserable."

"Something's different with you," Sammi said. "Usu-ally by now you've prowled the perimeter and chosen your conquest, but tonight you haven't left the bar."

She was right. Daniel had been so focused on Sydney that he hadn't made a single connection. He hadn't met a woman, townie or tourist he could take home tonight. It hadn't even crossed his mind until Sammi mentioned it.

But now wasn't the time. He had the feeling, by the way the mayor was watching Sydney, he was waiting for the best moment to make trouble for her.

"The way Daniel's been watching Sydney, I'd say *she's* his next conquest," Jon said.

"Just watching her back," Daniel told him. "She didn't want to come here, but I persuaded her. I told her she needed to get out."

"Well, she seems to be having a good time," Sammi said.

The song Sydney and the rookie were dancing to ended and he walked her to the bar to buy her a drink.

"Yeah, but the mayor is up to something," Daniel said. "I can feel it." And he wasn't going to leave her to fend for herself. She was still too vulnerable.

"So you're going to protect her?" Jon asked.

"That's what I do," Daniel said with a shrug. "Protect and serve."

"Don't you mean protect and *service?*" Sammi said, and the men laughed.

"Like I said, she's just a friend." But if she wasn't a single mom, wasn't his neighbor, wasn't his *friend,* he would seduce her in a heartbeat. He didn't think it would be difficult.

"So you wouldn't mind if I asked her out?" Jon said.

Daniel shrugged. "Nope."

"Aren't you a little young for her?" Sammi asked.

"She doesn't strike me as the cougar type." Jon gave her playful shove.

"So what do you think the mayor will do?" Jon asked.

"I'm not sure." But they didn't have to wait long to find out. The mayor's girlfriend excused herself to the ladies' room, and the second she was out of sight Harris was crossing the brewery, weaving through the crowd, heading for Sydney, who stood at the bar talking with one of the deputies' wives. Luckily Daniel was closer and reached her first.

"Let's dance," he said, linking an arm through hers.

She out let a surprised, "Oh!" as he half walked half dragged her to an open spot on the edge of the dance floor. A slower song was playing, so he tugged her close, and the way Sydney fell against him, unsteady on her spike heels, said the alcohol was going to her head. And instead of tensing the way she usually did when he touched her, she actually relaxed against him.

"Thank you for forcing me to come with you tonight," she said, smiling up at him. "I can't remember the last time I had so much fun."

Man, she had a sexy mouth. And he was seriously considering kissing her—just to see if she would let him—when he glanced past her and realized they were about to have company.

"Bogie at twelve o'clock," he said, nodding in the mayor's direction.

Sydney turned to look, cursing under her breath. But

then she gave her head a shake and said, "You know, to hell with him. I'm having too much fun to care."

"Sydney," the mayor hissed, stopping beside her and Daniel. "A word."

"No," Sydney said, sliding her arms up and around Daniel's neck.

The mayor's brow rose. *"Excuse me?"*

"She said no," Daniel told him.

Harris shot daggers with his eyes. "When you address me, *Deputy,* you address me as sir."

When hell froze over, maybe.

"What are you doing here, Sydney?" the mayor demanded.

"What does it look like I'm doing? Hanging out with friends."

"You don't have any friends." And it was clear he took a great deal of satisfaction in that assumption.

"You keep telling yourself that," Sydney said, leaning even closer into Daniel, until her breasts were nestled firmly against his chest.

Harris's eyes narrowed and he said, "Are you *drunk?"*

"Why do you sound so surprised? You're the one telling everybody what a lush I am. I'm just living up to my reputation." She looked up at Daniel and said, "Do you know the only times I ever drank while we were married? It was when Jeff wanted sex, and getting tipsy was the only way I could stand to have him touch me—"

"That's enough!" Harris thundered, grabbing Sydney's

arm and yanking hard. If Daniel hadn't been holding on to her she probably would have tumbled over.

Daniel was two seconds from decking the son of a bitch, when Harris's girlfriend appeared at his side, looking like a wounded doe, and said, "Jeffy, what are you doing?"

At that point people had stopped dancing and were watching, and maybe Harris realized that he'd just come off as the jealous ex-husband who was still pining for his wife, because he dropped Sydney's arm so swiftly she fell back into Daniel.

He gave Sydney one last furious glare and then stormed off, his girlfriend scurrying after him.

"Did he hurt you?" Daniel said, examining her arm.

"I'm okay," she said, looking a little rattled. "I guess I hit a nerve, huh?"

"You realize he just assaulted you. You should file a police report. You have a bar full of people who will corroborate." If Sydney had done the same to Harris, Daniel didn't doubt she would be cuffed by now. The bastard deserved a taste of his own medicine. He deserved to be humiliated.

"It's not worth it." She slid her arms back around his neck, pressed the length of her body against his. He realized that watching her stand up for herself had made him hot as hell.

He eased her into his arms, forcing himself to keep his hands north of her waist. When what he really wanted to do was cup her behind and grind himself against her.

Nope, not gonna happen. She was drunk, and he knew better. Fooling around with a woman who couldn't consent was a line even he wouldn't cross.

She gazed up at him with heavy-lidded eyes, a smile on her full, glossy mouth.

God, he wanted to kiss her.

"Is he watching?" she asked.

Daniel skimmed the crowd and saw Harris standing by the bar, eyes on Sydney, looking ready to spit nails. "He's watching. And he's pissed. You made an ass out of him."

"No, he did that to himself."

Good point.

She grinned up at him and said, "You want to give him something to be really pissed about?"

"What did you have in mind?"

She pulled his head down and brushed her lips across his.

Oh, man.

It was far from passionate, yet suddenly his pulse was racing. He'd kissed a lot of women, but he couldn't recall ever *feeling* it like this.

Sydney's eyes fluttered open and she gazed up at him, lips parted in surprise. Whatever it was he'd felt, apparently so had she.

Time seemed to stand still, the air between them so thick it was damn near impossible to draw in a full breath. Then she curled her fingers into the hair at the nape of his neck, her nails raking over his skin, and he almost groaned. Before he knew what he was doing, his lips slanted over hers and he captured her mouth. With not only her ex, but most of Daniel's friends watching, after he'd been so adamant about not dating Sydney.

Wrong, wrong, wrong. This was so wrong. He needed to stop this before it went any further. Before he couldn't stop.

He broke the kiss and pressed his forehead to hers. They were both breathing hard.

She gazed up at him, eyes glazed. "You want to get out of here?"

Shit.

Don't do it, Daniel. This is a bad idea.

But before he could stop himself, he was leading her to the door, walking so fast she could barely keep up with his longer strides. The only thing he could think about was getting her home and naked. He wouldn't allow himself to consider anything else. Like the inevitable consequences.

When they got to his truck he helped her in and then walked around. He'd scarcely made it into his seat before she was in his lap, straddling him, her lips crushed against his. He'd never been with a woman who kissed more passionately. Who tasted so sweet. She wound her arms around his neck, grinding her lower body against him. God, she was hot. But not only was this bordering on indecent, it was a logistical nightmare. There was a good reason he hadn't had sex in a car since he was a teenager.

"Not here," he said, lifting her from his lap and depositing her on the seat beside him. "Buckle up."

She snapped her seat belt in place. "Drive *fast*."

He drove the speed limit.

"Is what you told your ex true, or were you just trying to piss him off?" Daniel asked. "Did you really have to drink to be able to stand him touching you?"

"It's true."

He tried to imagine being with someone who physically repulsed him, and couldn't even fathom it. "If it was that bad, if you were so unhappy, why did you stay?"

"For Lacey. I didn't want her to grow up in a broken home."

So she had sacrificed her own happiness for her daughter's. "And how did that work out for you?"

Sydney let her head fall against the seat and sighed. "It was a disaster. I should have left him years ago."

He was probably asking too many questions, but he couldn't help himself. "Has there been anyone since him?"

She shook her head.

"So you haven't enjoyed sex in how long?"

"Well, even in the beginning it wasn't great. It wasn't awful, either. He was just always a...selfish lover, I guess. More concerned with his own pleasure than mine. So the last time I had really fantastic sex was probably... seventeen years ago."

That was just *wrong,* but it didn't surprise him. For Daniel, giving a woman pleasure was what turned him on, what fed his own pleasure. And Sydney was long overdue.

He stopped at a red light on the edge of town, reached over and hooked a hand behind Sydney's neck, leaned in and kissed her, quick and deep.

They lived only a few miles off the downtown strip, so it didn't take long to get there. And this time she didn't wait for him to open her door. She hopped out and landed unsteadily on the concrete driveway. Daniel told himself that it had more to do with her heels than her level of intoxication.

"My place," Sydney declared. "Lacey is sleeping at a friend's house. I want to be here if she calls."

A reminder of why he avoided single moms. Too much baggage. Tonight he would make an exception.

But what about tomorrow?

He shook away the thought and followed Sydney to her back door. She fumbled with her keys under the dim porch light, then dropped them when she tried to get the key in the lock.

Not drunk, just clumsy.

He grabbed the keys, found the right one and opened the door. They'd barely made it inside and her arms were around his neck, her lips locked on his. She started to drag him backward toward her bedroom, clawing his T-shirt free from the waist of his jeans. She stumbled and he had to catch her or she would have landed on her behind. She wasn't just a little tipsy. She was hammered.

He cursed silently. As much as she *seemed* to want him, her judgment was impaired.

He couldn't do this.

They got to her bedroom and she dragged him inside, shoving the door closed behind them. Because that's what moms did. They closed doors so kids didn't see things they shouldn't. Like their vulnerable mother getting it on with the bachelor next door.

Shit.

He *really* couldn't do this.

He took her by the arms, unwound them from around his neck. "Sydney, stop."

She looked up at him, brow wrinkled with confusion. "What's wrong?"

"We can't do this."

"What? *Why?*"

"Because you're drunk."

"So what?"

"You aren't thinking clearly. And there are at least a *dozen* other reasons this is a bad idea."

"But...I *want* to."

"I do, too, more than you will ever know. But I can't. I'm sorry."

Sydney looked absolutely crestfallen. And he cringed when, in the moonlight shining through her bedroom window, he could see the sheen of tears in her eyes. "But..."

"Take a second to consider what you're doing."

She looked up at him, then glanced around the room, as if she was wasn't quite sure how she had arrived there. Then the reality of what she had been about to do seemed to hit home.

"You're right," she said softly. "This would have been a mistake."

She lost her balance and had to sit on the edge of the mattress. "I guess I did have a lot to drink," she said, and it seemed to take extra concentration to form the words clearly. "I'm feeling a little woozy."

"Why don't you lie down."

She complied without question, crawling up the mattress to lay her head on the pillow.

"You want help with your boots?"

She nodded.

He gently tugged them off and set them by the closet where she wouldn't trip over them. "Anything else?" he asked, hoping she wouldn't ask him to help take her clothes off. Even he had limits. But she shook her head.

"I'm tired," she said, her eyes drifting closed.

Not ready to leave her just yet, he sat on the edge of the mattress beside her, smoothing back the loose tendrils of hair framing her face. She made a soft, contented sound.

"Thank you for taking me out tonight," she said drowsily. "I really did have a good time."

"We'll do it again."

"I'd like that."

He kept stroking her hair until she fell asleep, then he let himself out of her house, locking the door behind him, and went home. He walked in and switched on the light beside the couch. It was so quiet.

All he'd thought about for a month was getting a moment to himself, but now that he'd gotten it, he felt awfully...*alone.*

OH. MY. GOD. Her mom was doing it with the cop next door!

Lacey sat on her bed, unable to believe what she'd

heard last night, and listening for signs that her mom was waking up. For all she knew, *he* could still be in there. Last night, when she'd heard them come into the house and go straight to her mom's bedroom, Lacey had put her headphones on and blared her music. Whatever they were doing in there, she didn't want to hear it. And probably the only reason she'd heard *anything* was that her mom thought she was still at Veronica's house.

Lacey didn't know if she should be shocked or happy for her or totally grossed out. Moms were not supposed to have flings with next-door neighbors. At least not *her* mom. She'd never done a spontaneous thing in her life! Of course, if she was going to do it with anyone, why not a man as hot as Deputy Valenzia?

She thought of her father's little bimbo, who had the brain capacity of a fruit fly, and actually felt proud of her mom for picking someone like Deputy Valenzia. Maybe she deserved to have some fun after all the crap Lacey's father put her through. It was a bit gross and very weird. But maybe women her mom's age had needs just like men did, and it had probably been a really long time since her mom had sex.

Well, not anymore.

She wondered if this meant she would have a cop for a stepdad.

The phone rang and Lacey dug for the extension under a pile of clothes on her bedroom floor. "'Lo."

"Hi, angel, it's Daddy."

Lacey rolled her eyes. She hated it when he used the word *daddy,* as if she was still five. Like it would make her hate him any less. And she wasn't anyone's *angel*. "What's up?"

"Something came up and I won't be able to have you over today."

Boo hoo. Well, Lacey hadn't wanted to see him anyway. And she was sure that the "something" was the bimbo.

"Since you're out of school later this week, I thought I could come and pick you up Thursday and we'll spend the afternoon together. I'll take you shopping."

Wasn't that typical of her father, always trying to buy her off. Well, she didn't want anything from him.

"I can't," she said. "I'm going job hunting. I want to help Mom since her new job probably doesn't pay as much."

"What new job?"

No thanks to you, Lacey thought bitterly. "She's working for our next-door neighbor. Deputy Valenzia. She's his nanny."

"Since when?"

"She starts Monday."

There was a long pause, then he said, "Let me talk to her." His voice sounded funny, like he was really angry. Was it possible that he was mad that her mom was working again? Lacey knew he was the one who got her fired from her old job.

A sly smile curled her mouth. It was payback time. "You can't talk to her now, she's still in bed."

"It's after eleven!" he said, sounding appalled. "Wake her up."

No way. "I can't."

"Why?"

"Because she has...company."

"*Company?* Who?"

"Who is that on the phone?"

Lacey spun around to see her mother standing in the bedroom doorway in her robe, hair rumpled, last night's mascara smeared under her eyes.

"Is that your mother?" her dad barked. "Put her on *immediately*."

"It's Dad," she said, holding out the phone. "He, uh, wants to talk to you."

Her mom rolled her eyes and took the phone. "What do you want, Jeff?"

Lacey could hear her dad shouting through the phone, and wondered if maybe this hadn't been such a hot idea after all.

Her mom's mouth fixed into a thin line, then she flashed Lacey a stern look. "She said I was doing *what?*"

Yeah, definitely a bad idea. Her mom looked pissed.

"Ice Queen? Yeah, sure, I'll pass on the information."

Lacey cringed. She'd heard her dad call her mom the Ice Queen more than a few times, and accuse her of being closed off emotionally. Her mom might not have been the most affectionate person in the world, but being married to Lacey's creep of a father, who would be? Lacey couldn't even remember the last time she saw her parents kiss, or even hug each other. In fact, she didn't know if she'd *ever* seen them do that.

"Frankly, Jeff, whether I am or not is none of your

damned business." There was more yelling and some distinct swearing, then her mom laughed. "Bad influence? Are you kidding me? This coming from Mr. I'm-cheating-on-my-wife-with-my-twenty-two-year-old-assistant?"

Whoa! Her mom really must have been mad to blurt that out. Lacey knew about her dad's affair with the bimbo—and the ones before that—but her mom had never said a word about it in front of her.

There was another pause, then she said, "And explain to me exactly *how* this is different?"

Apparently her dad had every intention of doing just that, because Lacey heard more swearing and yelling. Then her mom did something she'd never done before. Right in the middle of his rant, she slammed down the phone.

"The man's ego knows no bounds," she grumbled, rubbing her temples as if she had a headache. Of course, listening to Lacey's dad shout would give anyone a headache.

The phone started ringing again almost immediately. "Do not answer that," her mom warned.

The machine picked up on the fourth ring and Lacey could hear her dad shouting from the other room. Her mom turned to her, and Lacey waited for the explosion.

Instead, she said calmly, "Why did you tell your father I'm having an affair with Daniel?"

"That's not what I said."

"No, but you implied it."

"Well, you are, aren't you?" Lacey said defensively. "Why not tell Dad?"

Her mom sat on the edge of her bed beside her, shoving a pile of unfolded laundry to make room. "First off, no, I am *not* having an affair with Daniel. And even if I was, that would be my private business."

Lacey wasn't used to talking about this kind of stuff with her mom. Usually she would just say something snotty and walk away. But for some reason, she knew it would be wrong to do that this time. She'd been a real pain lately and her mom had been putting up with it for the most part, but Lacey could tell her patience was wearing thin.

"I heard you guys come in last night. I'm not stupid. I know something was going on in there."

"I thought you were staying at Veronica's."

"I had a headache, so I came home." She twisted the ring on her thumb. "It's okay. I was kind of grossed out at first, but I'm not upset or anything. I think you *should* start dating."

Her mom sighed. "What you heard last night was Daniel helping me in because I had too much to drink. Then he left."

"Oh."

"I appreciate that you're okay with me dating, honey, but if I do, it won't be our next-door neighbor. Or a man I'm working for."

"He's really hot."

She sighed. "Yeah, he is. I'm just not ready to date anyone yet."

Her mom slipped an arm around her and Lacey rested

her head against her shoulder, like she had when she was little. It was nice. Sometimes she wished she was little again. Things had been so much easier then. Her parents hadn't hated each other as much. And her mom hadn't been so sad all the time. Maybe if she started dating she'd be happy again.

"From now on, let's keep my personal business personal, okay?"

Lacey nodded. "Sorry."

"You should get ready. Your dad will be here soon."

"No, he won't. He canceled again."

Her mom squeezed her shoulder. "Oh, honey, I'm sorry."

"I'm not. I didn't want to see him anyway. I hate him."

"He's made lots of mistakes, but he's still your father. He deserves your respect."

"You always told me that to earn respect you have to give it. Well, he doesn't respect *me*. All he does is make fun of the way I look."

"He's just…"

"An opinionated, egotistical jackass?"

Her mom tried to hide a smile. "But he's here."

She knew her mom was referring to her own dad, who took off when her mom was only thirteen. Lacey had never even met her grandparents. Her grandma supposedly had mental issues, and her mom hadn't seen her since she left Michigan. Lacey couldn't imagine going that long without seeing her parents. Even if her dad was a tool.

"I have an idea," her mom said. "Since neither of us has plans, why don't we go to the lake? The water will still be a bit cold, but we can work on our tans. We could pack a picnic lunch."

Normally Lacey would consider going to the lake with her mom pretty lame, but she had the feeling her mom needed the company. "Sure. That sounds like fun."

"You could invite Veronica if you'd like."

Lacey shrugged. "That's okay. It can just be us this time."

"By the way, I'm sorry I said that about your father. About him cheating."

"It's not like I didn't already know, Mom. Everyone knew."

"I know."

"And just so you know, if you change your mind and want to date Deputy Valenzia—want to date anyone—it's really okay with me. I want you to be happy."

"Thanks, honey. I love you."

For some stupid reason, tears brimmed in Lacey's eyes. "I love you, too, Mom."

CHAPTER SEVEN

SYDNEY WISHED she was one of those lucky people who blacked out after drinking too much. Because then she wouldn't remember, in precise detail, the way she'd thrown herself at Daniel last night.

What the hell had she been thinking?

Simple, she hadn't been. She'd had so much fun, and so much to drink, she obviously hadn't been thinking straight. For the first time in…well, she couldn't even remember how long, she'd felt *alive*. And attractive. And when she'd kissed Daniel it had honestly only been to make Jeff mad, which, she now realized—now that she was sober—had been incredibly childish. But once she'd started kissing him, she didn't want to stop. And obviously, neither did he. She was just relieved he'd had the good sense to apply the brakes before they went too far.

And what had possessed her to bring him home? The fact that Lacey had heard anything filled her with shame. As if the kid wasn't confused enough already. If she and Daniel were in a committed relationship, that might be different. But Lacey needed stability in her life, and she wouldn't get that thinking her mom was having one-night stands with men she hardly knew.

Sydney glanced over at her daughter in the passenger

seat, her headphones on, eyes closed, her nose pink from the sun. She'd been stunned when Lacey agreed to go to the lake, and even more surprised when she hadn't insisted on bringing a friend. And though Sydney had pretty much spent the entire afternoon sleeping off a killer hangover, it had been nice to spend the day together, just the two of them. They didn't do that nearly often enough anymore.

Jeff had called while they were at the lake to say that he'd rearranged his schedule and he would be picking Lacey up in half an hour, and he'd been furious when Sydney told him it was too late. What the hell did he expect, that after he had repeatedly canceled their plans, Lacey would drop everything on a moment's notice to see him? That she would sit around waiting for him to acknowledge her?

Sydney had sworn to herself the day Lacey was born that she would always be there for her daughter, would always protect and support her. She never wanted Lacey to know what it was like to feel abandoned or ignored. Though now she wondered if everyone would have been happier if she had never married Jeff. Not only had it done Lacey no good to see her parents so unhappy, but Sydney had wasted years of her life with a man she didn't love.

But it wasn't too late to start over. Until last night at the bar she had forgotten what it was like to feel attractive, to feel *wanted*. And knowing that Lacey was okay with it made Sydney wonder if it was finally time to put herself out there. To consider a relationship with a man.

Any man but Daniel, that is.

Speaking of Daniel, Sydney thought, she was going to have to stop at his place and apologize for last night. For the way she threw herself at him. Not that he'd seemed to mind, not at first anyway.

As if she wasn't uncomfortable enough around him. Now every time she looked at him, she was going to remember how it felt to be pressed against him, the taste of his lips, the spicy scent of his skin. And she would always wonder what it would have been like if he hadn't said no.

When they pulled into the driveway, the sun was just beginning to set, and as soon as the van stopped Lacey opened her eyes.

"Home already?" she said, yawning.

Sydney handed her the keys. "Unlock the door. I'll get the stuff from the back."

She got out and walked around to the rear of the van, but before she could grab the beach bag, Lacey called to her.

"Mom, did you forget to shut the back door when we left?"

She circled around to find Lacey standing by the back door, looking worried. "No, why?"

Lacey pointed. "It's not closed anymore."

She was right; the door was standing ajar. Had Sydney forgotten to pull it shut? She'd had her arms full when she'd left. Was it possible that she just hadn't pulled hard enough? It did tend to stick.

Lacey reached for the knob and Sydney said, "Wait!"

It certainly wasn't worth taking a chance. If someone had broken in, they could still be there.

"Come with me," she said, waving Lacey over.

"Where?"

"Next door."

Amazingly, Lacey didn't argue.

They crossed the yard to Daniel's house and Sydney knocked on the front door. He opened it, April on his hip, looking surprised to see them there. And her worry must have shown, because immediately he frowned and asked, "What's wrong?"

"We just got back from a day at the lake and the back door is open. I *think* I closed it when we left, but I thought, just in case…"

"You did the right thing." Daniel held the door open. "Come in."

As soon as they were inside he handed April to her. Without a word, he disappeared into his bedroom and emerged a second later holding a gun. Lacey's eyes went wide, and Sydney's heart stalled.

"Stay here with the baby," he said.

"What are you going to do?" Sydney asked.

"Make sure no one is in your house."

"Shouldn't we call the police?"

He looked at her funny. "I *am* the police."

"I know, but shouldn't you call for backup or something?"

"Don't worry, okay? Just stay here with April."

He stepped outside and Sydney watched out the front window as he crossed the yard to her house, gun at his side, until the van blocked her view.

"She's cute," Lacey said, gesturing to April. "Can I hold her?"

"Sure, honey." She handed April over. The baby tangled her fingers in Lacey's hair.

Sydney turned to keep looking for Daniel. She hoped that if someone had been in her house, they were gone now. Or maybe she just hadn't shut the door all the way. Maybe she was making a big deal out of nothing.

"I've never seen a gun that close before," Lacey said, sounding a bit awestruck.

"Me, neither, honey."

"It was weird."

Actually, it was kind of…sexy. If she could set aside the worry that Daniel might be in danger. Maybe she should have just called 911 instead of dragging him into this.

Sydney paced anxiously by the window. Nearly fifteen minutes passed before he reappeared, the gun tucked into the waist of his jeans.

She met him at the front door. "Well?"

"No sign of forced entry or an intruder."

"So I overreacted and bothered you for nothing."

"It's better to be safe than sorry."

She still felt stupid. She'd just been so paranoid since the "Fred" incident.

"Can I go in the house now?" Lacey asked.

"Sure, honey." She took April from her. After Lacey was gone, she told Daniel, "I'm really sorry about this."

"Don't be."

"I feel like I'm taking advantage of you. Just because

you're a cop, it doesn't mean I have the right to come running to you whenever I have a problem."

"It's okay, Sydney. I honestly don't mind."

In her experience, that was the kind of thing people said, but didn't actually mean, but he seemed sincere. He was so *nice* to her. She wasn't used to that. With Jeff everything had been about what *he* needed or wanted.

She couldn't help but feel she should be waiting for the other shoe to fall. For Daniel to show his true colors. After all, she'd known him less than a week. The guy was bound to have flaws. Jeff had seemed nice at first, too.

Or maybe she should consider the possibility that Daniel was exactly who he appeared to be.

She handed April to him and said, "I should get home."

"I was just about to put her down for the night then I thought I'd sit on the porch and have a beer. Care to join me?"

She really should get home. After last night, maybe it wasn't such a good idea to be alone with him.

"I should get home," she repeated.

"You have plans?"

"No, but…"

"So you would rather sit home alone than have a beer with me?"

No, she would much rather be with him, and maybe that was the problem. But she didn't want to hurt his feelings, or seem ungrateful for his help.

"A beer sounds good. Although, we might be more comfortable on my deck. I have a patio set and citronella torches for mosquitoes. You can bring the baby monitor so you could hear April."

"Sounds much more luxurious than my porch. I'll put her to bed then meet you out back."

At least at her own house Lacey would be there, eliminating the opportunity for hanky-panky. Never in her life had she entertained the idea that her teenage daughter would be her chaperone.

While Daniel got April settled, Sydney crossed the lawn to her house. She decided to leave their beach gear in the van for now, and went to her bedroom to change, since she was still wearing her bikini under her shorts and tank. She considered taking a quick shower to wash away the sunblock and beach grime, but she didn't want to keep Daniel waiting. It wasn't as if he would be getting close enough to tell, anyway.

She changed into a soft cotton sundress, readjusted her ponytail and smoothed on some lip gloss.

Not great, she thought, checking her reflection, but passable.

She stopped by Lacey's room to tell her she would be in the yard, and found her sound asleep in bed. Lying in the sun all day must have wore her out. Not to mention that she may not have slept well, thinking her mom was in the next room with the neighbor.

She closed Lacey's door behind her. So much for a chaperone.

It was already dark as she went out to the deck. Daniel was already there, leaning against the railing, holding two beers. He'd lit the torches and they shed dim light across his profile. He was looking out over her yard, and when he heard her he turned and smiled. "I thought maybe you changed your mind."

"Sorry, I had to change."

He twisted the tops off both beers and handed one to her. She took a long swallow and leaned on the railing beside him. The night was clear and the moon hung full and unusually bright in the eastern sky. "Pretty night."

"Yeah. Glad I'm not on duty, though."

"Why?"

"Full moon. Brings all the nuts out."

She couldn't tell if he was serious or teasing her. "I thought that was an old wives' tale."

"Nope. People really do act weird during a full moon."

Maybe that explained her behavior last night. The moon made her do it.

"So, should we set a limit for you?" he asked. "Now that I know what happens when you drink too much."

Suddenly Sydney's cheeks were on fire. She'd been hoping they could just forget about last night. She should have known Daniel wouldn't let her off that easy. He had an aggravating habit of liking to talk about things, and a predilection toward brutal honesty.

Her philosophy was far less complicated. Why talk when it was so much easier to sweep issues under the rug?

But she could feel his gaze boring through her. She picked at the label on her beer, so she wouldn't have to look at him. "I'm *really* sorry about that."

"If you'll recall, I wasn't complaining."

"No, but it was wrong to throw myself at you. And in front of all your friends. I can't even imagine what they must think."

He took a swig of his beer. "That I'm a lucky guy."

"They think we're…?"

"Wouldn't you?"

She cringed. "I'm sorry."

"I think Jon wanted to ask you out."

"Deputy Montgomery? Seriously?"

He nodded. "He thought you were hot."

"What is he, twelve?"

"Mid-twenties, I think."

She swallowed a mouthful of beer. "I guess I should probably thank you."

"For…?"

She kept her eyes on her bottle. "Stopping things before they went too far. Not taking advantage of me. I'm not normally that…aggressive. It's just, well, it's been a long time. Since I've…you know…"

"Had sex?"

She nodded, her cheeks on fire again. He was probably used to talking about this sort of thing. He oozed sexuality from every pore, and she was the ice queen. But the things he could probably do to make her melt…

"Had I been sober, that never would have happened," she said.

"Are you saying that you weren't turned on by me specifically? I was just…convenient?"

She could tell by his grin that he was teasing her again, and she couldn't resist playing along. "Pretty much."

His grin turned sly, and his eyes smoldered like hot coals.

Uh-oh.

"Are you sure about that?" he asked, setting his beer on the railing and sliding closer.

Oh, no, what had she done? "P-pretty sure."

"So if I did this…" He took her beer from her and set it next to his, then he held her hand in his much larger one, palm up, and with his other hand, gently traced a finger down the center of her palm.

Oh, dear God.

This time her flush had nothing to do with embarrassment.

"Anything?" he asked.

"Nothing," she lied, hoping he didn't hear the waver in her voice, and also hoping he *did*. Whatever it took to keep him doing exactly what he was doing. Because as petrified as she felt, and as wrong as this was, she *liked* it. She liked his teasing grin and the heat in his eyes. She wanted to touch him, feel his hard muscle, run her fingers through his hair. But what if he was only playing with her? What if he didn't really want her?

She felt paralyzed by indecision.

"So why is your heart pounding?" He reached up and caressed the pulse point at the base of her throat, which only made it beat faster. She tried to think of some clever comeback, but her mind had gone blank.

"No comment?" he asked.

She opened her mouth to say something, anything, but then he stroked her throat with the backs of his fingers and a sigh slipped out instead. His eyes locked on hers and she went limp all over.

"You don't have the slightest clue how beautiful you are, do you?" he asked. "What did he do to make you so unsure of yourself?"

It was what he hadn't done.

Sure, at first Jeff had been amazing. He'd showered her with gifts and affection. He'd made her feel that she was the most important thing in his entire world. But it hadn't lasted. She wanted to believe that Daniel would be different, but experience had taught her otherwise.

"You're going to make me prove it, aren't you?" he asked, but the heat in his eyes told her he didn't mind in the least.

Oh, please do, she thought, even though she was terrified. But Daniel was leaning in to kiss her, and she could feel herself being drawn closer, like a moth to a flame.

His lips hardly brushed hers, teasingly, and before she knew what she was doing her arms were around his neck, pulling him down.

It had to be the full moon, she rationalized, but then he deepened the kiss, and she stopped thinking altogether. She could only feel. The sensual rhythm of his tongue, the strength of his arms as they pressed her against his body, his beard stubble scratching her chin. Good Lord, did the man know how to kiss.

His hands slid slowly down her back to cup her behind, and when he held her tightly, there was no doubt that he wanted her just as much as she wanted him.

But was it really Daniel she wanted, or the idea of

Daniel? Someone who would treat her well, be nice to her. Maybe she wasn't ready to be with *anyone* yet. Especially when she knew this was an impossible, dead-end relationship.

What was she *doing?*

She broke the kiss and pushed gently at his chest.

"We need to stop doing that," she said.

"Why?"

"Because I don't date cops, and you don't date single moms."

"Who said anything about dating?" he asked with a wicked grin.

"Daniel, I'm serious."

"So am I."

She shot him a look, and when he realized she meant it, he sobered. "Why?"

She untangled herself from his arms and backed away. "Because I can't do this. Not with you."

"You can't tell me you're not attracted to me."

"That doesn't mean it's a good idea. When it comes to relationships, we want very different things."

"You want a commitment?"

Yes, and it was obvious by the edge to his tone, he didn't. "I wasted fifteen years in a lousy relationship. I have a chance to start over now, and this time I refuse to compromise." She took his hand. "The past few days have been great. You've been a wonderful friend. I don't want to lose that."

He squeezed her hand. "You won't. And I didn't mean to pressure you into anything."

"How could you have known, with all the mixed

signals I've been sending out? Maybe *I* didn't even know."

"But you do now."

And it was because of him. He forced her to take a good hard look at her life. The way she had been wasting it. She'd been happier this past week, felt more like *herself,* than she had in years.

"Well, the message is clear this time," he told her. "From now on, we'll just be friends."

He actually sounded disappointed, which made her feel good and rotten at the same time. What woman didn't enjoy being wanted? And she wanted him, more than she had ever wanted a man before. She knew that sex with Daniel would be nothing short of thrilling.

But she wasn't in it for the sex. At least, not entirely. She wanted someone kind and gentle and responsible. And safe. A man who was interested in going the long haul, and maybe having another baby. She wanted a real relationship.

Daniel wanted none of those things.

"This isn't the beer talking, is it?" he asked.

"Not this time." Maybe the beer made it easier to say the words, but the feelings were genuine.

So why did she feel so darned unsure of herself?

CHAPTER EIGHT

LACEY WAS crazy nervous.

She stood outside the door of AAA Landscape, the company Daniel's sister Angie owned, wondering if she was wasting her time. According to her mom, Angie was looking to hire a few high school kids for the summer. But would she be willing to take on someone with zero job experience? She would just have to hope that Angie took pity on her and gave her a chance. Her only other option was a summer job at the resort, which would mean having to rely on her mom for rides, or at a fast-food restaurant, which would totally suck.

But she couldn't get any job if she didn't at least try. She pulled open the door and stepped inside. She figured she'd find an entire staff, but there was only one woman sitting at a desk doing something on a computer.

At the sound of the door opening, the woman looked up and Lacey knew she had to be Daniel's sister. She was dark like Daniel and really pretty. She had long, glossy black hair pulled back in a ponytail that hung halfway down her back.

She smiled. "Hi, there, can I help you?"

"Hi," Lacey said. "My mom is Sydney, your brother's nanny, and she said that you said you were hiring."

"You're Lacey!" she said, rising to shake her hand.

Her grip was so firm it actually hurt a bit. "Your mom said she would send you by. I thought maybe she forgot, or you found a job somewhere else."

"Well, school just let out yesterday, and before that I had finals to study for."

"Right! Of course. Your mom did mention that." She shook her head and laughed. "I'd forget my head if it wasn't attached. Come on in and grab a seat. I'll get you an application."

Lacey sat down while Angie rifled through a file cabinet. She seemed a little flighty, but super nice. She found what she was looking for and shoved the drawer closed with her hip. She handed the application to Lacey and gave her a pen.

"I don't have much experience," Lacey said, toying with the ring in her brow—the stupid thing still hurt like hell. "Just some babysitting. Is that okay?"

"Sure." Angie propped her feet up on the desk. "We all have to start somewhere. Don't even worry about that part. I just need your personal info and your social security number."

Did that mean Angie was actually considering hiring her?

As Lacey was filling out the form, the door opened behind her, and a deep voice said, "Hey, Mom, we're leaving to do the strip mall."

Lacey turned, her eyes traveling way, way, *way* up to the face of the guy standing behind her, and for a second she could swear her heart actually stopped beating. This was Angie's *kid?* Her mom had mentioned that Angie had a seventeen-year-old son, but for some reason, Lacey had pictured a scrawny, nerdy kid. There was nothing nerdy about this guy.

He was *totally smoking hot*.

"Jordan, this is Lacey," Angie said. "Her mom is April's nanny."

"Hey," he said, barely even glancing at her. He looked a lot like his mom. And Daniel, too, and he was just as big. Definitely a jock. And though she didn't usually go for the athletic type, she would make an exception. If she didn't already have a boyfriend, that is.

Jordan took off his baseball cap and swabbed his sweaty forehead with the hem of his T-shirt, exposing a totally ripped and tanned stomach.

Shane? Shane who?

Lacey realized that she was practically drooling and forced herself to look away.

"I got a call from the Petersons," Angie told Jordan. "They're throwing an engagement party for their son and they want to totally revamp their yard by next week."

"Seriously?" Jordan said, sounding exasperated.

"Yeah, and they're paying handsomely, so try to see how many people you can talk into working overtime. Tell them they'll get time and a half."

"I'll see what I can do." He turned, his heavy work boots thudding on the linoleum floor, and Lacey resisted the urge to check out his ass. She doubted it would be anything but perfect.

"How are you doing with that application?" Angie asked.

"Um, done, I think."

Angie took the application and scanned it quickly. "Ever plant flowers or shrubs, do any landscaping?"

"I've helped my mom with the garden and she makes me cut the lawn."

"You free this week, starting tomorrow?"

She nodded. "Sure."

"Awesome! I'll have Jordan pick you up on his way to the Petersons in the morning."

"Does that mean I'm hired?"

Angie laughed. "Of course you're hired. The job starts at minimum wage."

"Okay." Minimum wage was better than no wage.

"Do you own a pair of work boots?"

"I have hiking boots."

"That'll do. And wear jeans. It's supposed to be close to ninety degrees tomorrow so bring lots of water."

"Okay. Cool." Lacey rose from her chair. "I better go. My boyfriend is waiting for me outside."

"Don't forget, 7:00 a.m."

"I won't. Thanks, Angie!"

Out in the parking lot Shane was lying on the hood of his Camaro smoking a cigarette, a pair of sunglasses shading his eyes. As she made her way to the car, she saw a man across the street and immediately recognized him as her dad's creepy handyman. That was weird. She could have sworn she saw him outside the school two days ago when classes let out.

He didn't look her way, or act as if he knew she was there, so she wrote it off as a coincidence.

"It's about time," Shane said as she approached, rolling to his feet. "How long does it take to fill out one stupid application?"

"It's not stupid," she snapped, her excitement instantly overshadowed by a wave of prickly irritation. He still didn't take any of this job stuff seriously. "They hired me. I start tomorrow."

Shane ground his cigarette into the pavement with his running shoe and opened the driver's side door. "What am I supposed to do while you're working?"

Like I care, she thought, getting in the car. He was being such a jerk, maybe she didn't want to see him anymore. Maybe it was time to find a new boyfriend. One who treated her with respect.

One who was tall, dark and *hot.*

Shane started the car and peeled out of the parking lot. Lacey grabbed the edge of the seat to keep from tumbling over.

"I still don't get why you need a job."

"I told you a million times, I want a car."

"So ask your dad to buy you one."

She snapped her seat belt into place as he rounded another sharp turn at excessive speed. "I don't want anything from him. I'll earn it myself."

He shrugged. "Hey, whatever. Just don't expect me to sit around waiting."

"Is that a threat?"

Shane didn't understand. His parents practically trampled over each other to buy him everything he asked for. At first she had thought it was pretty cool dating a guy with the hottest car and money to burn, but he didn't have any ambition.

Not that she was in the market for a marriage-material type of guy. But sometimes she got so bored with Shane she wanted to scream. He treated her as if she didn't have a brain half the time—and seemed to like it that way!

Lacey thought about seeing Jordan in the morning, and got a squishy feeling in her stomach.

"Lacey!"

"Huh?" She turned to Shane.

"I asked if you want to go to your house. It's too hot to be outside."

She shrugged. "Yeah, sure. Whatever."

"Are you dense or something? I called your name three times and you didn't even hear me."

It was amazing how much he sounded like her dad just then. But she didn't care.

"Sorry." She turned her head and looked out the window, unable to suppress a smile. "Just thinking about my new job."

DANIEL PULLED HIS CRUISER into the AAA Landscape lot next to the shiny new BMW parked there. He didn't have to run the plate to know who it belonged to.

He was still holding out the hope that the guy was a passing phase. That Angie had learned her lesson with her ex-husband, Richard. Although Daniel seriously doubted it. He'd spent the better part of his adolescence and his entire adult life keeping his twin out of trouble. Guiding her away from stupid decisions.

Lately it had been a full-time job.

He got out of the cruiser and pushed through the door

into the building. Angie was sitting at her desk and Jason Parkman, her "boyfriend," sat perched on the edge of the desk in golf attire, leering at her bare legs.

Daniel was instantly on alert. Jason was too...*perfect*. His clothes were never wrinkled, his shoes never scuffed, and Daniel often wondered if he cut his prematurely salt-and-pepper hair on a weekly basis because it was always the exact same length. Even worse, the man was perpetually nice—nice to the point of being irritating. And though he never flaunted it, Daniel knew he came from a wealthy family, just like Richard.

Richard had been a nice guy, too, and possessed that same air of casual sophistication. He'd once told Daniel he fell in love with Angie's quirky personality and admired her spunk and free spirit. But he'd had a dark side no one knew about. At least Angie had gotten a pretty fantastic kid out of the deal. And since Jordan only saw his dad a couple of times a year, Daniel had been the only consistent male role model he'd had.

As Daniel came through the door Angie looked up and flashed him a nervous smile. "Hey, Danny."

"Hello, Daniel." Jason slid off the desk, extending a hand to shake. Daniel gripped it firmly.

"Jason," he said, being polite for Angie's sake.

"How is Sydney today?" Angie asked with that teasing look he'd grown accustomed to this past week, since he was getting it from everyone, despite how many times he insisted he and Sydney were just friends.

"You wanted to see me?" he asked his sister.

"That's my cue to leave," Jason said, leaning over to kiss Angie, making Daniel glower behind his sunglasses.

He could have the decency not to do that when Daniel was around.

"Bye, sweetie," she said, watching him leave with a sappy, lovesick expression that made Daniel want to vomit. The man had her completely snowed.

"Bye, Daniel. See you next weekend."

"Don't even say it," Angie said after he was gone.

"I didn't say a word."

"Yeah, but you want to. I just don't get why you don't like Jason. *Everyone* else likes him. Even Abbi, and she hates *all* men!"

Which was why it sucked being the only man left in a family full of gullible women.

"I've been seeing him for six months. When are you going to accept that he and I are serious? I love him."

He would never accept that, because this relationship wasn't going to last. "He said he would see me next weekend. What did he mean?"

Angie took a deep breath and blew it out. "Okay, now I don't want you to get mad—"

Daniel groaned and rolled his eyes. When she started a conversation that way, he knew it would be bad. "What did you do?"

"Just listen," Angie pleaded. "I probably told you that Jason has a house on the coast, off the cove in Stillwater."

"Yes, you've told me."

"Well, he's invited the family to come stay for the weekend."

"The *whole* family?"

"Mom can't come because she has to work, but Beth

and Dee will be there. And Jordan, of course. And I said you would come, too."

"Angie—"

"Danny, *please*. It would mean so much to me. And I know you won't believe it, but it will mean a lot to Jason, too. He loves me, and he knows how unhappy it makes me that you disapprove. He wants to give you a chance to get to know him."

She got up from her chair and grabbed his hands. "Please, Danny? You know you owe me. Big-time."

He hated it when she played the guilt card. She *had* been an enormous help when April had been dumped in his lap. He hadn't had a clue what he needed to buy or what to feed her. Angie had saved his behind. And April's.

"Pretty please," she said. "Do this for me and I swear I'll never ask another favor from you ever again."

Well, they both knew that was crap. But this weekend obviously meant a lot to her. And maybe if he did go, it would be an opportunity to somehow to drive a wedge between her and Jason.

"How long would we be gone? Because if you recall I've taken an awful lot of time off work lately."

"We would drive there Friday evening after work and come back Sunday afternoon."

"When?"

"A week from this Friday." She steepled her hands under her chin. *"Please."*

Daniel cursed under his breath. He knew he was going to regret this… "Fine, I'll go."

She squealed and threw her arms around his neck.

"Thank you so much! You're the best brother in the world!"

"All right, all right," he said, disentangling himself.

"This is going to be so much fun! Dee is going to bring Jake and Beth is bringing Louis."

"So everyone is bringing a date but me?"

Her smile evaporated. "Um, yeah. I guess so. I hadn't really thought about that."

Wonderful. So everyone would pair off and he'd be left with April and Jordan? Sounded like a blast.

"You can bring someone, too."

"Who? I haven't been on a date in over a month. I'm not seeing anyone."

"Hey, why don't you ask Sydney?"

"Sydney and I are *not* dating," he snapped. And it had been hard as hell keeping his hands to himself the past few days. He didn't know why but he found her... fascinating. The way she looked, the way she moved. The scent of her skin. He couldn't stop thinking about touching her. And it was obvious she wanted him, too.

And a commitment.

What was it with women? After suffering through such a rotten marriage, why would she want to do that to herself again?

"Ask her anyway, as a friend. She can bring Lacey. That will give Jordan someone his own age to hang around with. And Sydney can help you with April."

That actually wasn't a bad idea. But would she agree? Maybe if he made it part of the job, and offered to pay her.

"Why aren't you dating her, by the way?" Angie asked. "I've seen the way you look at her."

"How do I look at her?"

"Like she's a nasturtium, and you're a bee looking to do some pollinating."

"Nice," he said, shaking his head, unable to suppress a laugh.

"And you two were going at it pretty hot and heavy on the dance floor Friday night."

"I'm not dating her because she just wants to be friends."

"That's never stopped you before."

"Yeah, well, this is different." He could see Angie was waiting for him to elaborate. "She wants a real relationship."

She gasped. "Oh, horrors! A *real* relationship?"

"I don't want to hurt her."

"Again, that's never stopped you before."

"Sydney is different. I…I like her. She deserves better than someone like me."

"If you like her that much, have you considered the possibility that you might be ready to have a real relationship?" He glared at her, so she shrugged and said, "Or not."

"I'm happy being single. Indefinitely."

"And childless?"

The way she said it made Daniel feel like an ogre, when he was only doing what was best for April. "April will be better off with her real family. With two people to raise her. I can't give her what she needs."

"How's the search going?"

Not well, unfortunately. "The P.I. called yesterday and said that he may have tracked down a cousin of

Reanne's in Utah. But to know for sure, he has to actually go there, and that will cost more than I can afford right now."

"I would think that if Reanne had wanted this cousin to have April, she would have made sure that happened."

"I want to exhaust all possibilities before I resort to adoption."

Angie's tight-lipped silence said she didn't approve. Nor did his mom, or his other sisters. But if they were asked to take in a virtual stranger's baby, he'd bet they'd react the exact same way.

And he wasn't going to rehash his motivations all over again, because Angie wouldn't listen anyway. "I have to go."

"Let me know what Sydney says so I can tell Jason."

She had better hope that Sydney agreed to go, and if she didn't, Daniel was able to find someone else who would. Because he'd be damned if he was going by himself.

"I SAID *stop!*" Lacey shoved Shane as hard as she could and watched him roll off the couch and land with a thud on the den floor. He'd gone too far this time—*way* too far.

He scrambled to his feet. "What's the matter with you?"

She glared at him as she refastened her shorts. "What's the matter with *me?* Are you dense? I asked you to stop about five times."

I accept your offer!

Please send me two free Harlequin® Superromance® novels and two mystery gifts (gifts worth about $10). I understand that these books are completely free—even the shipping and handling will be paid—and I am under no obligation to purchase anything, ever, as explained on the back of this card.

About how many NEW paperback fiction books have you purchased in the past 3 months?

❑ 0-2
E9KY

❑ 3-6
E9LC

❑ 7 or more
E9LN

❑ I prefer the regular-print edition
135/336 HDL

❑ I prefer the larger-print edition
139/339 HDL

Please Print

FIRST NAME

LAST NAME

ADDRESS

APT.#   CITY

STATE/PROV.   ZIP/POSTAL CODE

Visit us online at
www.ReaderService.com

▲ © 2010 HARLEQUIN ENTERPRISES LIMITED. ® and ™ are trademarks owned by and/or its licensee. Printed in the U.S.A.

H-SR-01/11 ◀ Detach card and mail today. No stamp needed.

He looked confused. "Every girl says stop. That doesn't mean she actually *wants* you to stop."

Was he serious? "I actually wanted you to stop!"

"Why?" He was completely mystified. He honestly couldn't believe she didn't want him groping her. "What's the big deal?"

She picked one of his tennis shoes up off the floor and threw it at him, nailing his right arm.

"OW! Lacey!" The other shoe went flying and connected with his left leg. "Lacey, stop it! What is your problem?"

"We are so done," she said.

Disbelief played across his face. "You're *breaking up* with me?"

"I'm breaking up with you."

Shane pulled back his shoulders and puffed out his chest, which wasn't all that impressive considering how skinny he was. It made Lacey think of the way Jordan's tank top strained over all that muscle.

She should want her boyfriend to kiss and touch her, but when Shane did, she just felt…uncomfortable. And the whole time he was kissing her today, she was thinking about Jordan.

"I could name a dozen other girls who would come running if I snapped my fingers," he sneered.

She picked up his shoes and shoved them at him. "Then start snapping."

"You bitch," he snarled, and for a second he looked as if he might hit her. She'd seen her dad look at her mom that way before. He'd never actually hit her, but there were times when she thought he'd probably come close.

So Lacey did what her mom would do. Instead of backing away, she stood her ground, looking Shane right in the eye.

If he'd been considering violence, he changed his mind. He grabbed his shoes and stormed down the hall toward the front door. "You'll regret this."

"I seriously doubt that," she mumbled, following him. When he was out the door she shut it behind him, fell against it, and exhaled. Thank God that was over. Maybe she should have felt bad or guilty for wounding his pride, but all she felt was relieved. For weeks she'd been unhappy with Shane, but she hadn't let herself admit it. Maybe she'd thought that a jerk of a boyfriend was better than no boyfriend at all.

Until she met Jordan. Until his voice sent chills up her arms, and she looked into his deep, dark eyes and felt all tingly inside. Of course, Jordan didn't know she existed, but that was about to change. She would make him notice her.

She was good at that.

Lacey heard the side door open and had this sudden vision of Shane sneaking back in to beg her forgiveness. Then she heard her mom calling her.

"In here," she answered.

Her mom appeared in the living room doorway holding April who was gnawing on a teething ring, drooling all over the place. "I just saw Shane leave and he looked upset. Did you guys have a fight?"

"We broke up." She walked over to her mother and

took April from her. April bounced excitedly, reaching for her hair and yanking it.

"Oh, sweetheart, I'm sorry." Sydney folded Lacey in her arms until they were all bunched up in a three-way hug. Both she and April smelled like soap and baby powder.

"Actually, I'm fine. It was my decision." She backed away and noticed her mother's shirt was drenched. "Jeez, Mom, you're all wet."

"Huh?" Sydney looked down at her shirt. "Oh, I was giving April a bath. It's like trying to wrestle an octopus. I came home to change. Why did you break up with Shane? He seemed nice."

"Let's just say he has hearing problem."

Her mom frowned. "What do you mean?"

"He doesn't listen when I say *no*."

Her brows rose. "Oh. Well, good for you, then."

"Besides, he was pissed about me getting a job and he would have given me a hard time about it."

"You went to see Angie today?" She gestured for Lacey to follow her to the bedroom.

"I filled out an application."

Her mom handed April over then she stripped down to her underwear, tossing the wet clothes into the hamper. "And?"

Lacey sat on the bed with April, who promptly tried to climb out of her arms. "She hired me."

"Oh, honey, congratulations! When do you start?"

"Tomorrow. Early."

"Do you need a ride?"

"They're picking me up."

Sydney nodded, then turned to her closet. She chose a loose-fitting blue sundress and pulled it over her head.

"Why are you wearing that?" Lacey asked.

"Because it's comfortable."

"But you have a really nice figure. You should show it off."

Her mom gave her a look. "This coming from the girl who wears jeans three sizes too big?"

"Because I *don't* have a figure."

"And who am I showing it off for?"

Lacey shrugged. "No one in particular."

"I'm babysitting, not looking for men."

Well, with Daniel around she didn't have to look far. She had to know that he was gorgeous, and even Lacey could see that he liked her. What possible reason could she have *not* to date him? It would be kind of cool to have a cop for a stepdad.

"Just so you know, Daniel's working the afternoon shift tonight so I won't be home until after eleven," her mom said.

She shrugged. "Whatever. I'm probably going to bed early anyway."

"I just didn't want you to worry."

No, she didn't want Lacey to think she was over there playing tonsil hockey. "You know, I really like Daniel. And I can tell he likes you. *A lot.*"

Her mom shot her a stern look. *"Lacey!"*

"What? He *does*."

"We're just friends."

"Do you make out on the dance floor at Moose Winooski's with *all* your friends?"

Her mom's cheeks turned bright pink. "Who told you that?"

So it was true. "This is a small town, Mom. People talk."

"Despite what we did or did not do at Moose Winooski's, Daniel and I are just friends. End of story."

"Well, Veronica said he looks like he would be a good kisser."

"He's a little old for Veronica."

"Ew! Gross, Mom. She didn't say *she* wanted to kiss him. She was just…speaking hypothetically."

Which reminded her, she had to call Veronica and tell her she'd dumped Shane. Veronica would be happy, since she thought Shane was a narcissistic tool.

"I should get going." Her mom took April from her. "You know where I am if you need me."

Lacey got up and followed her to the side door. "Mom?"

Her mom stopped and turned. "Yeah, honey."

"I don't mean to nag about you and Daniel. I just…I want you to be happy. You deserve it."

Her mom smiled. "Thank you, sweetie. And I want you to know how proud I am of you for standing up for yourself with Shane. For not letting him pressure you into something you're not ready for. There will be other guys. Guys who treat you with the respect you deserve."

"I know." In fact, she was hoping she'd met one already.

CHAPTER NINE

SYDNEY STEPPED OUT the side door and started across the lawn, thinking that, for all the grief Lacey gave her sometimes, she was one hell of a sweet kid. Then she saw that Daniel's police cruiser parked in front of his house and sighed.

Not again.

This was the second time he'd been by today. He'd been by twice yesterday, too. In fact, he'd been by the house at least twice *every* day that week. As if he was keeping tabs on her or something. He'd said he trusted her, but now she wasn't so sure.

Monday he'd had been gone only two hours when he came back home, claiming to have forgotten a form he needed to give his boss. She'd believed him, and even bought his excuse when he showed up again later that afternoon to "grab a soda since I was in the neighborhood." Tuesday, he'd supposedly forgotten his wallet when she was almost positive she'd seen him take it with him in the morning. Then he'd stopped by around one "for a bite to eat." But he'd mostly just played with April, and had barely touched the pizza Sydney had reheated for him.

Yesterday morning, he said he'd spilled coffee on his pants and needed to change them, and though there *was* a stain, she suspected he'd done it on purpose to have an excuse. Then, yesterday afternoon, she'd taken April grocery shopping and he had appeared in the parking lot as she was loading the van. He said he happened to be driving by and saw her, but she had the feeling he'd actually followed her there.

Maybe, being a cop, he just naturally mistrusted people. But it was beginning to get on her nerves.

Even so, it didn't stop the warm, wistful feeling she got every time he walked through the door. It didn't stop her from constantly second-guessing herself, and questioning her decision to keep their relationship platonic.

Every one of her instincts was telling her that even though Daniel said he didn't want to settle down, *their* relationship would be different somehow. But she was also sure lots of women had thought that. Right up until the minute he broke their hearts.

What if she fell in love with him and ended up brokenhearted like all the rest?

And what if she didn't? What if she was different? What if he fell in love with her, too?

Was it worth taking a chance? Worth the risk of being hurt?

What she needed was a sign. She needed proof that he was capable of changing.

She opened the front door and stepped into Daniel's house. He stood in the kitchen, cell phone to his ear. She sighed softly, like she did whenever she saw him, imagining what it would be like to wrap her arms around his neck and kiss him hello.

When he saw her he snapped the phone shut and said, "Hey, where were you?"

"Next door. I had to change my clothes. I gave April a bath and she got me all wet."

He walked over and took April from her. "Hey, munchkin!"

April squealed happily as he gave her a big smacking kiss on the cheek. He may not have been ready for the responsibility of a child, but April was sure ready for him. She adored him. It broke Sydney's heart to think of her being shuffled off to strangers. Especially when Daniel was such a good dad. To see them together, no one would guess he was anything but a loving, devoted father.

"I gave her a bath this morning," Daniel said.

"I know, but she had rice cereal for dinner, and by the time we were finished she was wearing most of it."

"How's it going with the solid foods?"

"Good. But it's getting hard feeding her in her bouncy seat. She tries to crawl out. You're going to have to consider getting her a high chair. I'm sure you could find a cheap one at the resale shop in town."

"It's a lot to ask, but if I gave you the cash, do you think you could pick one up for me?"

It wasn't a lot to ask, considering Sydney would be the one who benefited the most.

"Sure. I'll go tomorrow." She moved to the kitchen to wash the dirty dishes and bottles. "What are you doing here?"

"I had a few minutes and I wanted to talk to you."

She tensed. In her experience, when someone said

they wanted to "talk" to her, it was never good news. Maybe he was finally going to tell her why he'd been checking up on her.

"Did I do something wrong?" she asked.

The question seemed to surprise him. "Of course not. Why would you think that?"

She shrugged, scrubbing the inside of a bottle with a soapy brush.

"I need to ask you a favor. And you are under no obligation to say yes."

"What kind of favor?"

"Angie has this boyfriend, Jason—"

"She told me about him. He sounds really nice."

"Yeah, well, he's invited our family to his place on the coast for the weekend. Dee and Beth are both going, and I said I would, too, and I thought maybe I could talk you and Lacey into going with us. I could really use your help with April. I'll pay you, of course."

Sydney rinsed the bottles and set them in the drain board. "Why would you pay me to come when your sisters are going to be there to help you? You said they adore April."

Daniel shifted, looking uneasy. There was definitely something he wasn't telling her.

"Is there another reason you want me to go?" she asked.

He took a deep breath and blew it out. "The thing is, Dee and Beth are both bringing their boyfriends. And Angie will have Jason."

Leaving Daniel the odd man out. A position she was willing to bet he rarely found himself in.

That made much more sense.

"When?"

"A week from tomorrow. We would leave after work and come back Sunday evening. I guess Jason's place is right on the water. And he has a boat."

"It sounds like fun. I'd love to go."

His brows rose. "Seriously?"

"Sure. Lacey and I could use a vacation. And you don't have to pay me."

"Sydney, you have no idea how much I appreciate this. And don't worry about Lacey being bored because my nephew, Jordan, will be there."

"I'm sure she'll have fun. And if you want, we can take my van and car pool. You and me and Angie and the kids."

"That would be great. You have no idea how much I appreciate this."

For some stupid reason, the fact that she'd made him happy made her feel good.

"Well, I'd better get back on the road," Daniel said, handing April over to her, seeming almost reluctant to let her go, to leave her alone with Sydney.

Ugh.

So much for those warm, fuzzy feelings. And though she hadn't intended to confront him, the words just spilled out. "Is there a reason you don't trust me?"

He looked genuinely perplexed. "What are you talking about? Why would you think I don't trust you?"

She set April in her playpen and gave her a toy to amuse herself with. "You stop by home every day. You follow me to the grocery store. What am I supposed to think?"

"Sydney, if I didn't trust you, I never would have asked you to watch April."

"Then why do you keep checking up on me?"

"I'm not checking up on you. I just…" He let his words trail off, and dragged a hand across his afternoon stubble.

"You just *what?*"

"It's stupid," he said.

"What?"

"For weeks I was with April 24/7. Now that I'm back to work…" He shrugged, as if he wasn't sure what he wanted to say.

But Sydney knew, and her heart climbed up and lodged in her throat. How had she not seen it before? "You miss her, don't you?"

"Maybe. A little," he admitted, looking so adorably confused she could have hugged him.

There was no maybe. For all his talk about not being ready to be a father, April had gotten under his skin. He cared about her. And if he couldn't go more than a few hours without seeing her, how would he cope if someone took her away for good?

He couldn't. Maybe he didn't know it yet, but April was *his.* He wouldn't be giving her up, no matter what he said. Sydney was sure of it.

Could this be the sign she'd been looking for?

She wasn't certain how it happened, but one second Daniel was standing several feet away, and the next her arms were around him. And oh, it felt wonderful. Her eyes closed as she laid her cheek against his chest. She flattened her hands across his wide, strong back, breathing him in, wishing she could crawl inside his skin to get closer.

"Whoa," he said, sliding his arms almost tentatively around her. "What's this for?"

"Because I wanted to," she said. "And because you looked like you needed it."

"If you had any idea how tough it's been not touching you this week, you wouldn't be getting this close to me."

His words thrilled and terrified her. And made it all too clear that this was exactly what she wanted. It just felt right. Besides, where was the fun in playing it safe? Hadn't she been doing that long enough?

"Or maybe you get some sort of warped thrill torturing me," he said. "In which case I might just have to retaliate."

"Maybe I *want* you to retaliate."

There was a pause, as if he was trying to decide if she was serious. "Maybe, or you do?"

"I definitely do."

"You said you want a commitment. I can't give you that. I don't do forever."

"I think what I really want right now is to have some fun. To feel like I'm getting on with my life." It wasn't completely true, but she knew it was what he needed to hear.

Another pause. "You're sure?"

She gazed up at him, into the inky depths of his eyes. "Why don't you kiss me and find out?"

This time there was no hesitation. He cradled the back of her head in his palm, making her tingle, and brushed a tender kiss across her lips. It was nice, but she could feel him holding back and couldn't blame him. She'd been playing emotional ping-pong for days. But even if she tried to resist him now, she couldn't. She wanted this too much.

She wrapped her arms around his neck, pulled his head down and kissed him deeply, so there would be no question in his mind what she wanted. The message was received loud and clear. Daniel moaned and pulled her against him, taking command of the kiss, and though he was clearly calling the shots now, she felt a thrilling sense of power.

He kissed away her doubts and her inhibitions, until Sydney felt herself going limp with need. And she *liked* it. She wanted *more*. But she had to pace herself.

She broke the kiss, bracing her palms against his chest, so breathless she felt light-headed. "Wow."

"Yeah. And for the record, changing your mind again is no longer an option."

"I won't. But I need to take this slow, Daniel."

"I can do slow." He pressed his forehead to hers. "It might kill me, but I can do it."

She smiled. She couldn't deny that it was a thrill to know he wanted her so much, it was going to be a struggle for him to keep control.

Daniel glanced up at the clock and cursed softly. "I'm on duty. I really have to go. What are you doing tonight around eleven-fifteen? You don't have to rush home for anything, do you?"

Lacey had mentioned going to bed early, so really, there was no reason Sydney had to be at home. "Nothing comes to mind."

"Maybe we could spend some quality time together?"

"We could do that."

"Then it's a date." He gave her one last deep, mind-numbing kiss, said goodbye to April and headed out the door.

This would be their first date. And despite the fact that they couldn't actually go anywhere, she had the distinct impression it would be a memorable one.

LACEY PACED in front of the living room window, her eyes fixed on the driveway.

"You're going to wear a hole through the carpet," her mom said from the kitchen doorway. She was still in her robe, drinking her first cup of coffee. And she looked exhausted, which Lacey was guessing had a lot to do with whatever was happening at Daniel's until 1:30 a.m.

Just a friend, huh?

"Are you nervous about your new job?" she asked.

"A little," Lacey said. Although it wasn't the work so much as the guy who was supposed to be picking her up.

"I'm sure you'll do just fine," her mom assured her.

A horn blared outside and Lacey's head swung back to the window in time to see a truck pulling into the driveway. She strained to see who was in the driver's seat. His face was concealed in shadow, but she could tell the person was male, and large.

"Sounds like your ride is here." Her mom stepped up beside her and looked out the window. The horn blared again. "You'd better go."

"See you later," she said, darting out the door and over to the truck. She grabbed the handle and flung the door open.

"Hi," a cheerful voice said. "You must be Lacey."

The guy's light brown hair was shoulder-length and he was really cute. But he wasn't Jordan.

"The one and only," she said, trying to disguise the disappointment in her voice as she hopped up on the seat. The interior of the truck was dusty, the carpet was filthy with clumps of dirt, and a pair of heavy work gloves lay on the seat between them.

"I'm Mike," he said, waiting for her to buckle her seat belt before he backed out of the driveway. "Did you know elephants are the only animal that can't jump?"

She blinked. "What?"

"It's true. Every other mammal can jump, but not the elephant."

"No kidding."

"Did you also know you can lead a cow upstairs, but not down?"

Lacey shook her head. "Nope, didn't know that, either."

"Most people don't." Mike glanced her way. "Is your hair always green?"

"Sometimes it's purple."

"Cool." He looked genuinely impressed, and he was

so cheerful, Lacey couldn't help but like him. Even if he wasn't Jordan.

"Did you know a duck's quack doesn't echo but no one knows why?"

She couldn't resist a smile. "You're just full of animal trivia, aren't you?"

"Not just animals. My brain is bursting with useless facts. It's a gift. Everyone on the crew calls me the Professor."

"Really? Who else is on the crew?"

Mike, the Professor, told her the names of all the crew members, which she couldn't help notice were almost all male, but he didn't mention Jordan.

"I met someone in the office yesterday—I think his name was Jordan," she hedged.

"He's Angie's kid. She puts him on whichever crew needs extra workers."

Mike chattered nonstop while he drove, soothing Lacey's frayed nerves. It was hard to be jittery around someone who kept her smiling constantly. But as they pulled up to the house where they were scheduled to work, and she saw Jordan leaning against another truck drinking bottled water, her heart went berserk again.

What was wrong with her? She'd liked guys before and never felt this weirded out.

"Jordan, I've got your new recruit," Mike called as they headed toward him. "Her name is Lacey."

Keep your cool, Lacey reminded herself. *Don't let him know you're interested.*

"Hi," she said in the detached, I-couldn't-care-less-what-you-think-of-me tone she used when she didn't want people to know what she was thinking. Jordan stared at her, his eyes slowly taking everything in from the top of her head down to her feet, until she felt naked. He was *huge*—at least a foot taller than her and twice as wide.

"We met yesterday," she added to break the monotonous silence, and still he stared at her. It wasn't a good stare, either. This blank stare said she was invisible and not even worth his time. A stab of anger suddenly replaced her nervousness.

"What's your problem?" she heard herself say.

"Do you have sunblock?" he asked, and she was so surprised he'd spoken, she lost her voice for a second.

"S-sunblock?" she stammered.

Jordan walked to the passenger door of the truck he'd been leaning on and reached in the open window, grabbing a small bottle off the seat. He tossed it to her. It was a tube of sunblock.

"Put it on, then meet me in the back." He walked away and she watched him, seeing several other workers already laying bricks at the side of the house. She turned to say something to Mike but he was unloading supplies from the truck they'd arrived in. He probably hadn't heard their conversation. If she could classify what they'd just had as a conversation.

"Hey," Mike said, coming up behind her with an armful of tools and a flat of petunias. "Did you know thirty-eight percent of America is wilderness, but Africa is only twenty-eight percent wilderness?"

"No, Mike, I didn't," she said, tossing the sunblock back through the truck window. She would rather cover herself in battery acid than use Jordan's sunblock. She also had the sinking feeling this was going to be the longest day of her life.

CHAPTER TEN

UNFORTUNATELY Daniel and Sydney's date never happened.

There was a huge fight at one of the less reputable bars in town and Daniel was held up at work until after 1:00 a.m. By the time he got home they were both too exhausted to do anything more than get ready for bed.

Sydney was disappointed, but it wasn't as if they didn't have the next night, and the next.

Though she hadn't fallen asleep until after 2:00 a.m., Sydney woke early the next morning to see Lacey off on her first day of her first official job. After she showered and dressed, she dumped the ingredients for spaghetti sauce in the slow cooker and set it to simmer. At eight, she locked up behind her and crossed the lawn to Daniel's house. Usually he unlocked the door in the morning so she could come in and take care of April while he got ready for work, but today it was locked. Figuring he'd probably forgotten, Sydney used her key and let herself in. She expected to smell coffee brewing, and hear the shower, but the house was dead quiet. Had he forgotten to set his alarm?

She cracked open his bedroom door and peered inside. Daniel was still in bed, snoring softly. If he didn't get up soon he was going to be late.

She slipped into the room and sat on the edge of the mattress. She wasn't sure what he was wearing under the sheet, but from the waist up he was naked. And *beautiful*. His chest was wide and muscular and sprinkled with dark hair, his stomach flat and defined. She considered taking a quick peek under the covers. She even reached for the edge of the sheet, but it seemed wrong to take advantage of him while he was sleeping.

She gently shook his shoulder instead. "Daniel, wake up."

He snapped awake instantly—no doubt a cop thing—looking up at her with bleary eyes, then glanced over at the clock. "Hey, what are you doing here? Is something wrong?"

"I came to watch April. I thought you had to be to work by nine."

He rubbed a hand over his face. "I thought I told you, I switched with Dave again. I'm working the afternoon shift. I'm sorry."

"Oh, that's okay."

"I would get up and make coffee, but April woke up at four and didn't go back down until almost six. I'm beat."

"Go back to sleep."

She stood, but Daniel grabbed her wrist. "You don't have to go."

"I should let you sleep."

"Why don't you slide in with me?" He pulled back the sheet and scooted over to make room for her. She was a little disappointed to see that he was wearing cotton pajama bottoms. But climbing into his bed? She wasn't sure if that was such a hot idea.

"Maybe I shouldn't."

"Nothing is going to happen." He patted the bed next to him. "Come on," he coaxed. "I like to cuddle."

What woman in her right mind could resist a sexy man who wanted to cuddle?

She climbed in beside him. He tucked her against him, spooning her so that her back was against his chest, his skin still warm from sleep.

Oh, this was *nice*.

It had been a long time since she'd snuggled in bed with a man. It was something she hadn't even realized she'd missed until now.

She must have been really exhausted because she fell right back to sleep. When she opened her eyes again Daniel was sitting on the edge of the bed, pressing soft, teasing kisses to her bare shoulder. He smelled like soap and toothpaste, and his hair was wet. He was dressed in jeans and nothing else.

"Wake up, sleepyhead," he said.

She stretched and yawned. "What time is it?"

"Eight forty-five. I guess you were tired. You passed out cold the minute you laid down."

"Why are you up?"

"I couldn't get back to sleep, so I got up and showered. And made coffee. I thought I could make us breakfast."

"Is April awake?"

He shook his head. "When she's up in the middle of the night she usually sleeps in late. She probably won't be up for another hour and a half at least." He leaned down, pressed a very soft kiss to her lips and then whispered against them, "Why? Did you have something other than breakfast in mind?"

He had no idea how tempting that was, considering how disappointed she'd been last night. But she wasn't sure how she felt about their first date taking place in his bed.

But he was kissing her lips and jaw, working his way over to nibble her ear. And she could feel herself melting.

"We're supposed to be taking this slow," she reminded him.

"We are," he said, kissing the curve of her neck. "We won't go any further than you want. Say the word and I'll stop."

In that case, maybe it wouldn't hurt to fool around a *little* bit. She beckoned him closer with a crook of her finger. He climbed in beside her with a grin.

For a while all they did was kiss, and kissing him was so nice, it was enough. He touched her face and rubbed her back, combed his fingers through her hair—nothing overtly sexual. But that didn't stop her from getting crazy turned on. After a while she was the one who was having trouble keeping her hands to herself. And she began to wonder if her plan was an unrealistic one.

She'd forgotten it was supposed to feel like this. So... *good.* For years, sex had been a duty. Something to tolerate, not enjoy. And then there had just been...nothing. No wonder her libido was slamming into overdrive. It hadn't been out to play in a *long* time. And Daniel wasn't doing enough playing.

"Hold on." She sat up to pull her shirt over her head, tossed it on the floor, then settled back down beside him.

He was grinning. "You trying to tell me something?"

"Maybe we don't have to go *quite* that slow." Although, with her past experience, she couldn't help but fear that she was destined to disappoint him. What did she know about pleasing a man? Near the end of her and Jeff's physical relationship, she hadn't done a whole lot more than just…lie there. And wait for it to be over. There had been a time when she enjoyed sex, but that was many years ago. She was sure, with practice, it would come back to her.

Daniel kissed her neck, her shoulder, then she felt him pulling her bra strap down and tensed.

He stopped and looked down at her. "Too much?"

Too much, too little. "I'm just a bit out of practice. I don't want to…disappoint you."

"Sydney, that isn't even a possibility. Besides, all you have to do right now is let me make you feel good."

Make her feel good? But what about him?

He slid the lace cup down, exposing her breast, and pressed an openmouthed kiss to her nipple.

She moaned and dug her fingers through his hair.

He bared the other breast and took it in his mouth, sucking hard, and for the life of her she could no longer recall why she thought going slow was a good idea. All she could process in her hormone-drenched brain was that she wanted *more*. She wanted to touch him. Feel him. But when she tried he intercepted her hands.

"Just you," he said.

He leaned over and pressed a kiss to the uppermost part of her stomach, then another just below it, then another, gradually working his way down.

He reached the waistband of her shorts, tracing a path across her stomach with his tongue, from one side all the way to the other. Sydney was so turned on, her thoughts were murky and unfocused, and the ache between her thighs was becoming unbearable. Daniel was going too fast, and not fast enough. And all she wanted was for him to touch her.

Expecting him to kiss his way back up to her breasts, she gasped when he pressed his mouth to the inside of her right thigh instead. The sensation was so foreign and erotic—and *good*—she gasped, jerking involuntarily.

He pulled back and looked up, as if he thought he might have gone too far. "Too much?"

Yes, but not in the way he thought. It was so good she felt completely out of control. And she *liked* it. If he stopped now she honestly didn't think she could stand it. "Don't stop."

He unfastened her shorts and sat up to tug them down. She lifted her hips to help him.

She expected him to lie back down beside her, but instead he lowered his head and kissed her again. This time higher, using his tongue to tease the crease where her body met her thigh.

She moaned and arched, her thighs falling open. Her wanton behavior should have embarrassed her, but she was walking the fine line between arousal and bliss, a place she hadn't ventured anywhere near in longer than she cared to remember. Daniel pressed her thighs even farther apart. The he pulled her panties aside and dipped his head.

The reaction was instantaneous. She cried out as pleasure wrenched through her. So perfect she wanted to sob, and laugh, and cry.

When she couldn't take any more, she pushed at his head, pulling her legs closed, saying breathlessly, "Too much."

Daniel grumbled a protest, trying to gently pry her legs apart. "Let me do it again."

"I can't."

"Yes, you can. One more time."

She shook her head. "Too sensitive."

She wasn't used to this. Her body had been ignored for so long, she needed to take her time. Besides, what about his pleasure? He must have expected something in return.

He started kissing his way back up her body, every touch of his lips causing a thrilling little aftershock. He settled beside her, but when she reached for the fly of his jeans, he stopped her.

"Don't," he said.

"Why?"

"I meant what I said. Right now all I want is to make you feel good."

SYDNEY LOOKED AT HIM as though he'd just beamed down from the mother ship. "But...what about you?"

Was he turned on? Hell, yes. And though his own body ached for release, he could wait. He *wanted* to wait. She needed to know that her pleasure was his top priority right now. That not all men were selfish when it came to sex. And making her see that was the only satisfaction he needed right now.

"Don't worry about me," he said.

"But—"

He smothered her words with a kiss. And for a while that was all he did. Kiss her and stroke her skin. Well, that and redirect her roaming hands as they strayed closer to his crotch. He finally got fed up and clasped her wrists together, pinning them to the mattress above her head.

She opened her mouth to complain, so he kissed her again, slow and deep. Not so easy to talk with his tongue in her mouth, was it?

She made a sound of protest and pushed against his hands, and if he'd thought for a second she wasn't enjoying it he wouldn't have hesitated to let go. But her struggle lacked conviction. In fact, being restrained seemed to fuel her arousal. After only a few minutes of kissing and touching her, he had her writhing and whimpering again. But this time he was going to make it last.

He slid his hand inside her panties to tease her, but the instant he touched her warm, dewy flesh, she shattered again. She arched against his hand, riding it out, until she moaned and crushed her legs together, gasping, "Please, no more."

She may have wanted to take things slowly, but her

body seemed not to grasp the concept. She was making this way too easy.

Sydney rolled on her side and curled against him, pressing her forehead to his chest, her breath coming in shallow bursts. "That felt...so good."

He reached around her back and flicked open the clasp on her bra. "You say that like we're finished."

"I am," she said, but she didn't stop him as he slid off her bra.

"I don't think so." He tossed her bra over his shoulder, then reached down to tug off her panties.

"I really can't," she insisted, lifting her hips so he could ease them down. For someone so adamantly against this, she was being awfully helpful. And he didn't doubt for a minute that he could talk her into making love. The weird thing was, he didn't want to.

No, it wasn't that he didn't want to. God knows he did. And if she had been any other woman he wouldn't have hesitated. But this was different. *Sydney* was different.

And maybe he was a little different now, too.

"You can," he said, kissing her before she could argue, determined to prove her wrong.

As many times as possible.

LACEY KNELT on the hard ground and planted flowers until her kneecaps felt like exploding. Then someone tossed her a pair of leather gloves and she was told to unload bricks and pass them to the bricklayers. This seemed to go on for hours, until her arms ached and her back had all but seized up from the bending and stretching. To top it all off she was soaked with sweat and felt like a boiled lobster.

When the crew stopped for lunch at one o'clock, she sat in the shade with the burger and soda Mike had bought her—since she forgot to bring money—and prayed someone would hit her in the head with a shovel and put her out of her misery.

Unaware of her silent suffering, Mike cheerfully informed her the original color of Coke was green.

Becky, the only other girl there, sat next to Lacey, showing off her various tattoos and piercings. A few in places Lacey would have preferred not to see. And despite looking like she could kick anyone's butt—even Jordan's—she was friendly.

Jordan's attitude hadn't changed all morning. He laughed and joked with everyone else and practically ignored Lacey. When he did speak to her, it was in that same cold, intolerant tone, and every now and then he would bark out an order or two.

When lunch was over she gathered up her garbage and limped to the trashcan. Turning back around, she ran face first into Jordan's chest.

"Watch where you're going," she snapped, but before she could back away he grabbed her arm and inspected it.

His brow furrowed and he shook his head slightly. "I gave you sunblock."

She ripped her arm out of his grip. "Who are you, the sunblock police?"

"I'll get the Professor to drive you home."

What? "I'm not going home."

"You're a mess. You're limping, sunburned and exhausted. Just admit you can't hack it and leave." He started to walk away.

Forgetting her various aches and pains, she stomped after him. "Is that what this is about? You're so chauvinistic you don't think a woman can do the job?"

Jordan just kept walking so she reached for his arm. The effect was like a static charge she felt all over. His skin was hot and slick with sweat, the muscles underneath hard as a rock.

Whoa.

He stopped and looked at the hand on his arm and then back down at her face, but the motion seemed to take an hour, as if the world were running in slow motion. She yanked her hand away and stuffed it into the back pocket of her jeans. "I'm fine. I can do the work."

He studied her for another eternity, and Lacey became aware that everyone else had abandoned what they were doing and turned to look at them. All the while Jordan kept those intense eyes glued to her face.

"Professor," he called suddenly and she jumped at the sound of his voice. "Take her to the truck, make her put sunblock on, then give her something easy to do."

He was letting her win this time, but not without humiliating her in front of everyone first. But she wouldn't let him or anyone else see how embarrassed she was. She lifted her chin, smiled up at Mike and said loudly. "If you're lucky, I'll let you do my back."

She hoped Jordan would hear, but he was halfway across the yard by that time.

Lacey spent the remainder of the afternoon picking up garbage, pulling weeds and gathering tools, with Jordan spouting occasional orders at her.

He wasn't rude or mean, just indifferent, and she had no defense against that. If she was rude, she'd seem childish. If she tried to evoke any reaction at all, good or bad, she'd seem desperate for his attention. No matter what she did she came out looking like an idiot, but for some reason she couldn't just sit back and be ignored.

By that evening she was relieved to be getting away from him. She couldn't imagine going through this day after day.

"Did you know an ostrich's eye is bigger than its brain?" Mike asked as they strolled to the truck. "And the longest recorded flight of a chicken is fourteen seconds."

"Professor!" Jordan called, jogging up next to them. "I need you to run to the office and drop off the equipment." He hitched his thumb in Lacey's direction. "I'll drive her home."

"Sure thing," Mike said, giving Lacey a sympathetic smile and a wink.

When they were alone, Lacey turned to Jordan. "I have a name, you know."

"Well, *Lacey,* unless you're walking, get in the truck."

She was so furious she probably *would* have walked if it hadn't been over five miles to her house. But with no other choice she got into Jordan's truck and sulked. He climbed in next to her and started the engine. "Buckle your seat belt."

"Make me."

He gave her one of those blank looks. "The truck doesn't move until your seat belt is on."

"I've got all the time in the world," she said, crossing her arms over her chest.

Jordan let out a quiet sigh and shook his head so subtly she almost didn't see him do it. Then he shocked her by leaning across the her and fastening the seat belt for her. In the few seconds he was stretched across her she could smell a hint of aftershave and the strong scent of a guy who'd worked in the sun all day. And she liked it. As a matter of fact, she liked it a *lot*. She wondered what he would do if she reached up and touched the soft jet-black curls peeking out from under the ball cap he wore. But as fast as he had pinned her, he straightened in his seat.

"Undo that and I'll put you over my knee," he warned tonelessly, putting the truck in gear and pulling away from the curb.

"Do you hate all females, or is it just me?" she asked.

"Who says I hate you?"

"Is *resent* a better word?"

"So, you assume I'm a woman hater?"

"It was just a question. Why do you care what I think, anyway?"

She saw his knuckles whiten as he gripped the steering wheel, and he didn't answer. Though she tried two more times to engage him in an argument, he fell back into that controlled indifference. He was infuriating— and fascinating. And as much as she wanted to hate him, he was getting under her skin and she couldn't figure out why.

When Jordan pulled up in her driveway, Shane's car was parked across the street. Shane was sitting on the hood waiting for her.

"Shoot." She instinctively sank lower in her seat. He'd texted her about fifty times that morning. She hadn't responded, so he started calling and leaving messages when she wouldn't pick up. It had gotten so annoying she'd had to shut off her phone.

Jordan looked at Shane then over at Lacey hunched low in her seat. "Problem?" he asked.

"I broke up with him and now he's stalking me."

"Is that the moron who was sitting in the parking lot the other morning?" he asked and Lacey nodded. "Figures you'd date someone like that."

"I told you, I broke up with him. He won't leave me alone."

"Well, then, you should be happy. You seem to like drawing attention to yourself."

"Screw you, Jordan." Shoving the door open with her shoulder, she stormed toward the house. Shane was behind her in a flash.

"Hey, Lace, stop. I want to talk to you."

He put his hand on her arm and she shrugged it off. "Not now, Shane, I'm tired."

"I just wanted to tell you, I'm sorry for whatever I did and if having a job is that important to you, I guess it's okay with me."

"Wow, that's awfully generous of you."

He grabbed her arm again, stopping her. "Lacey,

come on. You can quit playing hard to get. I said I was sorry." .

"Hey, pal, you want leave my girlfriend alone?"

She heard Jordan's deep voice behind her, and like that day in the office, the sound made her tingle. She and Shane both turned to see Jordan walking casually toward them, and for once that look of indifference was aimed at someone other than her.

"Who is this guy?" Shane asked, backing up a step. Jordan outweighed him by about fifty pounds—all of it muscle.

"You heard him, he's my new boyfriend," Lacey said, following Jordan's lead, trying not to stiffen when he slipped a sweaty arm around her shoulder and tugged her against his side. But she liked the feel of his arm there. She liked it so much she started to get that squishy feeling again.

"I have to go drop off the equipment but I'll stop by later," Jordan said, then stunned her by lowering his head and pressing his lips against hers. It wasn't a passionate kiss, but his lips were warm and soft, and she felt it *everywhere*. In places she never knew she was supposed to feel a kiss.

Kissing Shane was never like this.

When Jordan finally pulled away she was so dizzy she had to cling to him to keep from falling over. Shane hadn't hung around to watch, he was already halfway to his car.

"Thanks," she said, smiling up at Jordan, and was met by his usual cold, impersonal stare. As quickly as the grateful feelings enveloped her, they were gone.

"We're even," he said, then turned and strode toward the truck.

Humiliated, she held back a sudden well of tears. Foolishly, for that brief moment, she'd thought he liked her at least a little, but she had obviously been mistaken.

She was just about to turn toward the house when movement by the side of the house across the street caught her eye. She looked over just in time to see someone dart into the backyard.

Stupid nosy neighbors. They always looked at her like she was a freak. Not that she gave a damn what they thought of her. She didn't care what *anyone* thought of her.

And if she never spoke to that creep Jordan again it would be too soon.

CHAPTER ELEVEN

WHEN SYDNEY'S CELL PHONE rang later that evening and she saw an unfamiliar number, she almost didn't answer it, but Lacey had gone out with friends, so she picked up just in case.

"Hey, Sydney, it's Angie. Daniel's sister."

Angie was not someone she could easily forget. "If you're trying to reach Daniel, he's on duty."

"No, I called to talk to you."

"Oh." April grabbed the phone, so Sydney laid her in the playpen. "Is there a problem with Lacey."

"Oh, no, not at all! She's a supersweet kid."

Supersweet? "We are talking about my daughter. Lacey Harris? About five-three, blondish-green hair."

Angie laughed. "I really like her, and Jordan told me she's a hard worker."

"I'm glad to hear that."

"The reason I called was to tell you how happy I am that you're coming to Jason's. I know we'll have a blast. Even though Daniel doesn't like him."

"He doesn't?" Daniel was so easygoing, Sydney couldn't imagine him disliking anyone. Except maybe Jeff, but he deserved it.

"He thinks Jason is too much like my ex-husband,

Richard. But other than having money, they have nothing in common. Danny's just really protective of me."

The fact the he was so devoted to his family was a good sign. Not that Sydney was thinking in terms of a permanent relationship yet. At least, she was trying not to. But it was tough not to fall head over heels in love with the guy.

"I know you and Danny are just friends, and I respect that, so I'll only say this once. I think you would make a pretty awesome couple."

She wanted to tell Angie that they were kind of a couple now, but she wasn't sure what Daniel wanted his family to know, if maybe he wanted to keep their relationship quiet. Or if he thought they even *had* a real relationship. Maybe to him it was just a fling. Just sex. Although if that were true, wouldn't he have tried to actually *have* sex with her?

She certainly didn't want to push him, but this was something they needed to talk about. Just so she knew what to tell people if they asked.

"You're awfully quiet all of a sudden," Angie said. "Am I making you uncomfortable? I mean, for all I know you might not have those kinds of feelings for him. I'm sorry if I overstepped my bounds. I tend to get really nosy when it comes to Danny's relationships."

"I'm not uncomfortable. And as for my relationship with Daniel, it's…"

"Complicated?"

"Yeah."

"Well, as I'm sure you've probably figured out, Danny is a little commitment shy. But I always thought that would change when the right woman came along. And I don't mean to say that I think that's you. Or that it isn't you. I mean, unless you *want* it to be you. And if not, you know, just ignore me." Angie paused for a second then laughed. "I should shut up now."

"I understand what you're saying." Sydney had the feeling Angie was hoping she would either confirm or deny a relationship, but she didn't feel it was her place. And how could she when even she didn't know what was going on?

After she hung up with Angie, Sydney looked up local secondhand kids' stores, then she strapped April into her car seat in the van and they went in search of a high chair. She found a really nice, cheap one at the third store they tried. It was so cheap, she had enough money left over to get April a few toys, too.

When they got back to Daniel's house his patrol car was parked in the driveway and he was sitting on the porch drinking a soda. But this time instead of feeling defensive, Sydney knew he was probably on break, and there to see April for a few minutes.

She parked in her driveway and hopped out of the van.

"I'm not here to check up on you," Daniel called from his porch. But she already knew that.

"You want to help me?" she called back, walking around to open the back of the van.

He crossed the lawn, looking so good that, if they hadn't been in plain view of the entire neighborhood, she might have thrown her arms around his neck and kissed him. Then he stunned her when he hooked an arm around her, tugged her against him and proceeded to kiss her senseless. He tasted sweet, like the soda he'd been drinking.

"Hi," he said, smiling down at her. She couldn't see his eyes behind his mirrored glasses, but she was sure they were as lust-glazed as her own.

"Hi. What was that for?"

He shrugged. "Do I need a reason?"

Absolutely not, and he obviously didn't care who saw.

"I see you found a high chair," he said.

"You want to carry it inside while I get April?"

He grabbed the chair from the back of the van and carried it into his house, but when he tried to set it up, he became hopelessly confused.

"Here, let me show you." Sydney unfastened April from her car seat and handed her to Daniel. The baby went straight for his glasses, so he took them off and set them on the coffee table. Sydney showed him how to unfold and fold the high chair, how to raise and lower the height of the seat, how to remove the tray and hook it back on, and how to recline the seat for smaller babies who weren't quite sitting up yet.

"These things have changed a lot since my sisters were little," he said. "I don't recall them being so... complicated."

"I got a great deal. I want to scrub it down really well before I put her in it. Since you can't be too careful. And I had a few dollars left over, so I got her some toys, too."

"Thanks. I've been meaning to pick some up."

"It's no problem."

"I don't suppose…" He paused.

"What?"

"Well, I never anticipated having her this long, and she's been growing like a weed. All the clothes I got her are getting small."

She had noticed that. "You want me to get her some new clothes?"

"Only if you don't mind. Shopping was never part of the job description."

"I don't mind at all. I probably have a better idea of what she needs anyway. And I know where all the good sales are. Unless you'd prefer I buy resale."

He shrugged. "Whatever is easiest for you."

"Maybe we'll run out tomorrow after her nap." In fact, April seemed ready for bed now. Her lids were heavy and she kept laying her head on Daniel's shoulder and snuggling against his neck. Sydney was a little surprised she hadn't fallen asleep in the van.

"You want me to lay her down?" Daniel asked.

She was going to tell him no, that she could do it, but she had the feeling he really wanted to. "Sure."

She followed him down the hall and stood in the doorway as Daniel hugged and kissed April, then laid her in her crib.

"Good night, munchkin," he said, stroking her hair back from her face. Sydney watched, feeling the tiniest bit choked up. She was still convinced that, despite what he said, Daniel would never be able to give April up.

He closed the door on his way out and they walked back to the family room. "Before I forget, how would you feel about going out on a real date tomorrow? Since I covered for Dave, he and Sammi offered to watch April for the evening. I thought we could go to Moose Winooski's."

"That sounds like fun."

"However," he said, tugging her into his arms, "I feel compelled to warn you that the only man you'll be dancing with this time is me."

That was perfectly fine with her. He was the only man she wanted to dance with. "I suppose."

"It's possible the mayor might be there," he warned.

"He's in Hawaii with the bimbo." Although she almost wished he would be there, so he could see how happy she was. She'd had an unpleasant conversation on Tuesday when her lawyer sent his lawyer a bill for the locksmith. Jeff had called her from Hawaii, in the middle of his vacation, ranting about how she'd had no right to have any work done on the house without first getting his permission. Which they both knew was ridiculous. She reminded him that if his creepy handyman hadn't had a key, she wouldn't have needed to change the locks.

He launched into a tirade about Sydney's "boyfriend" and how she was losing sight of what was important, and that he was going to sue her for full custody, which again, they both knew was a load of crap. The fact that she sat quietly listening to his tirade, not reacting to his threats, seemed to infuriate him even more. After a bit more name-calling, he'd finally slammed the phone down. Her lawyer called a couple of hours later saying that they'd received a check for the bill. Which was what Jeff should have done in the first place.

Sydney didn't know why he expended so darned much energy antagonizing her. He had his bimbo girlfriend. Wasn't it time they both moved on? Although the truth was, he didn't annoy her nearly as much as he used to. She just...didn't care anymore.

"This is going to sound strange, but I feel kind of sorry for her," Daniel said.

"For who?"

"The bimbo. The way she follows him around like a puppy."

"You know what's really sick? I used to be just like her. But that's a story for another time. You have to get back to work."

He looked at his watch. "Yeah, I do. Can you stick around for a while tonight?"

She couldn't suppress a smile. "I'm sure we can arrange something."

He pressed a soft, lingering kiss to her lips. "I was thinking we could pick up where we left off this morning. If you think you're ready for that," he said.

Oh, she was *so* ready. The taking-things-slow plan had been a really dumb idea. She grinned and rose up on her toes to kiss him. "I'll see you at eleven-fifteen."

WHEN DANIEL LET HIMSELF into the house that night after work, Sydney was stretched out on the couch with the television on, April sprawled on her chest asleep. And when she looked up at him and smiled, he was struck with the oddest sense of...*peace*. He used to prefer coming home to an empty house, but he was getting used to having her and April there.

Although, in her formfitting tank top and cutoff shorts, with her hair pulled back in a ponytail, she looked a bit like a teenage babysitter. Which made him a degenerate for the thoughts he was having. But despite how she looked, he knew for a fact that Sydney was all woman.

She switched off the television and said, "Hi. How was work?"

"Busy. Bar fights, domestic disturbance calls, kids cutting loose. Typical Friday night stuff." He leaned over and kissed her, then April. "Couldn't she sleep?"

"I started her on applesauce tonight and it upset her tummy. But I think she's ready for bed now." She rose from the couch, cradling April close.

"I have to go change. You want me to lay her down?"

"Would you?"

"Sure. Why don't you grab us a couple of beers?"

"That sounds really good. It's been a long night."

He carried April to her room and set her gently in her crib, but she was sleeping so soundly a bomb could have gone off outside and she probably wouldn't have budged. He changed into jogging pants and a muscle shirt, shaking his head when he saw that Sydney made his bed again and the dirty clothes from his bedroom floor had been washed and folded. He'd told her repeatedly that she didn't have to clean his house and she especially didn't have to do his laundry. Or April's, for that matter. Yet every day he came home to a spotless house and clean laundry. It was as if she couldn't help herself.

Which was why he wasn't surprised to find her in the kitchen washing dishes.

"I'll do those tomorrow," he said.

"It'll just take a second." She never left his kitchen anything but immaculate. She gestured with her elbow to the beer on the counter by the fridge. "That's yours."

He grabbed it and took a long swallow. "Anything exciting happen after I left? Besides the tummy ache."

"Not really."

Sydney was totally focused on scrubbing baby bottles and not looking at him. She seemed...distant. Which Daniel was learning meant there was something on her mind. Growing up in a household with five sisters had trained him to be attuned to the subtleties of female emotions. Which he was sure had a lot to do with his past success with the opposite sex. "Something bothering you?"

She shook her head. "No."

And women accused men of not being open with their feelings. He stepped behind her and wrapped his arms around her waist, tugging her against his chest. "Come on, tell me."

She grabbed a dish towel and dried her hands. "It's nothing."

He turned her so she was facing him. "Talk to me, Syd."

"Angie called me today."

"Oh, God."

She laughed. "It was nothing bad. She just wanted to

tell me she was excited that I was coming on the trip. And she made it really clear that she thought we would be a good couple."

"That sounds like Angie."

"Well, I wasn't sure what to tell her. If I should even tell her anything at all."

"Why wouldn't you?"

"I wasn't sure if anyone was supposed to know."

"Is there a reason people *shouldn't* know? Are you worried how it will affect Lacey?"

"No, not at all. Lacey actually gave me permission to date you."

He shrugged. "So what's the problem?"

"Is that what we're doing?"

Daniel was beginning to understand what she was getting at, although for the life of him he didn't know why she wouldn't just ask him. "So what you're saying is, you want to know if we're dating, and if it's okay to tell people."

Sydney bit her lip and nodded.

"Yes, and yes. We're definitely dating, and I see no reason to deny it to anyone. Besides, after what happened at the bar last week, no one would believe me anyway."

"I know I probably seem very naive, but I haven't dated since I was eighteen. I've forgotten the rules, I guess."

"Well, you're lucky, then. Because I know them all." He grinned and tugged her in the direction of the living room. "And right now, the rules say it's time to make out on the couch."

CHAPTER TWELVE

DANIEL HADN'T BEEN KIDDING. He didn't let her dance with anyone but him at Moose Winooski's Saturday night. Not that she wanted to, and no one would have dared ask, with his arm looped around her waist all evening. It felt nice, since it had been an awfully long time since anyone had *wanted* to put their arm there.

She had been a little worried that people would treat her differently this time. Maybe last time they were simply being polite, but she was accepted just as easily as if they had known her for years. She felt as if she fit in. When she was married to Jeff, she'd always had the feeling she was an imposter, someone playing a role. Now she felt comfortable being herself. And the fact that she had been married to Jeff, and ceremoniously dumped him, made her something of a legend.

The more she talked with people, the more she began to realize just how many people didn't like him—and that a lot of people who seemed to like him, actually couldn't stand him. It had just been politics.

Their so-called friends hadn't been true friends at all. Their affection had been a political smokescreen, as she'd discovered after the divorce. What Sydney felt with Daniel's friends was genuine.

But what she found truly remarkable was the

acceptance she received from Daniel's family. They had been at the bar a couple of hours when Bethany and Delilah came in. They both had the same dark, striking features as Daniel and Angie. Apparently Angie had been singing her praises, and they were both eager to meet the new woman in their brother's life.

When Daniel moved down the bar to talk to Jon, Dee slid onto the empty bar stool beside Sydney. "So, Angie tells me you used to be married to the mayor."

"Yep."

Dee drained her glass and gestured the bartender for another drink. "He's an ass."

Sydney had been hearing that a lot lately. "Tell me about it."

"I probably shouldn't mention this, but he hit on me once, a couple of years ago."

Maybe that should have bothered her, but knowing Jeff hit on a woman, when there were so many others that he'd slept with, seemed insignificant. Sydney honestly didn't care any longer. "I'm sure he hit on a lot of women."

"I politely declined, and when I turned to walk away he grabbed my ass and made a disparaging comment about my heritage."

Dee smiled, as if the memory was a satisfying one. "I called him a fascist pig and threw my drink in his face."

Sydney laughed. She couldn't even count how many times she'd had that exact same impulse; she'd just never had the guts to follow through. "I wish I could have been there to see it."

"Not one of my finer moments. But it felt good. Danny wanted me to press charges. I figured wearing my scotch was humiliating enough."

Sydney had felt the same way when Jeff had grabbed her on the dance floor last week. He was his own worst enemy, and one of these days his temper was going to get him in trouble.

"Now, Danny," Dee said, nodding in his direction, "he's a good guy."

"I know." She glanced over at him and got a little shiver of excitement and attraction. And contentment. Everything in her said this was right. That Daniel was the man for her. Forever.

He must have sense her watching because he looked over and winked.

The bartender set a drink in front of Dee and she took a sip. "He must really like you."

"Why is that?"

"Because he's breaking all his dating rules to be with you. You're divorced and you have a kid."

"And I live next door."

"Exactly. And he tends to date women who are slightly…younger. Not that I'm saying you're old. It's just really nice to see him in a mature relationship for a change. He's hardworking, responsible and financially stable, but emotionally he's got Peter Pan syndrome."

"What do you mean?" Sydney hadn't seen any sign of that.

"He doesn't want to grow up. But I think having April around has forced him to reevaluate his life." She shrugged and said, "Like I'm one to talk. My longest relationship lasted less than six months. Our parents' marriage was so lousy I think we're all emotionally stunted to a degree. Except Angie. I swear she's made of Teflon. Things hit the surface and slide off."

Sydney felt an arm loop around her shoulder and turned to see Daniel.

"Care to dance?" he asked, pressing a kiss to her bare shoulder. Slow dancing with Daniel was like a form of foreplay. Lots of bumping and touching and kissing.

She slid down off the stool. "Love to."

He looked at his sister and frowned. "How many is that, Dee?"

She dug her keys out of her back pocket and handed them to him. "They're all yours, Deputy."

"We can drive you home later."

"That's okay. I'll catch a ride with Beth."

"Let me know if you change your mind." He took Sydney's hand and led her to the dance floor, tugging her close. "I thought you might need saving."

"What do you mean?"

"Dee has a tendency to get…*dark* when she drinks. And sometimes she says things she shouldn't."

"Like how my ex came on to her, and she threw a drink in his face."

Daniel shook his head and sighed. "Yeah, like that."

"It didn't come as a big shock. And it explains why you dislike him so much."

"I dislike him for a lot of reasons."

His sister Beth and her boyfriend, Louis, sidled up next to them.

"You take Dee's keys?" Beth asked Daniel.

"Yeah. What's her deal tonight, anyway?"

"Jake bailed on her. She thinks he's seeing someone else. He's her on-again off-again boyfriend," she told Sydney. "And it sounds like they're going to be off-again soon."

"Swell," Daniel muttered.

"Are you dragging her out of here or am I?"

"I told Dave and Sammi I'd be home by midnight." He glanced at his watch. "And it's eleven-thirty now."

Sydney could hardly believe it was so late already. The night had flown by.

Beth held out her hand and Daniel dropped Dee's keys onto her palm.

"Good luck," he said, and Beth rolled her eyes.

"Nice to have met you," she told Sydney. "We'll chat next weekend and I'll tell you some really embarrassing stuff about my brother."

"Goodbye," Daniel said, giving her a playful shove. When they were gone he told Sydney, "Sometimes I wish I had brothers."

"You guys are obviously very close."

"Things weren't easy when we were kids. We had to watch out for each other."

"Your parents' marriage was that bad, huh?"

"Both my parents had pretty volatile tempers. Occasionally the fights would get physical."

"Your dad was abusive?"

"It wasn't just my dad. My mom liked to throw things. One time, when I was in high school, they were fighting about something—probably money—and she threw a crystal vase at him. He wound up with a concussion and six stitches in the back of his head. My mom refused to drive him to the hospital, so I had to. He told the doctor in the E.R. that the vase had fallen from a high shelf and hit him. They separated a couple weeks later."

When he had said his parents' marriage was bad, she never realized *how* bad. Her parents' problems seemed mild in comparison.

"Did they ever hit you and your sisters?" she asked.

"My mom had an old breadboard she used for spanking us. My dad used the belt. But when I got older, he would just crack me in the mouth with the back of his hand."

"I couldn't imagine Lacey doing anything so horrible that I would be compelled to hit her. And for all Jeff's faults, he never so much as spanked Lacey. And he never raised hand to me." Physical violence wasn't in his nature. He'd been more of an emotional abuser. And a pathological liar.

"It stopped after the divorce," Daniel said. "It was as if they brought out the worst in each other. I figured we'd all learned from their mistakes. Then Angie married Richard."

"You didn't like him?"

"At first I did. We all did. They both seemed really happy, but then Angie started to change. My sisters kept telling me that something was wrong. I guess I didn't want to see it. I was friends with Rich. I couldn't believe that he could be mistreating her. And when I asked him about it he said that Angie was just having a hard time adjusting to being married. He basically blamed it on her, and I bought it. Then she showed up at my door one day with a split lip and a black eye. She was pregnant with Jordan at the time. Turns out the bastard had been knocking her around almost since the honeymoon."

The idea that someone would treat a woman as sweet as Angie that way made Sydney sick to her stomach.

"The thing I find the most ironic is that when my dad found out he flipped. He teamed up with a couple of his buddies from work and they paid Richard a visit. By the time they were done, he looked a hell of a lot worse than Angie did. And suffice it to say, he never laid a hand on her again. It's just common sense. If you're going to abuse your wife, don't marry the daughter of a cop."

"Your dad was a cop?"

"I never told you that?"

She shook her head. This Richard person must not have been very smart.

"Maybe Rich figured, since our parents got into it, it would be acceptable. He learned the hard way that wasn't the case."

"So Angie got a divorce after that?"

"Not right away. They separated and went to counseling for a few months. But he was offered a job in Washington state that he wanted to take, and there was no way Angie would leave her family, so they called it quits. The divorce was official when Jordan was six months old."

"And I thought it was bad that my parents ignored me."

He was quiet for a minute. Then he said, "You know what I just realized?"

"Hmm?"

"Besides my family, and a few close friends, I've never talked to anyone about this."

The idea that he trusted her enough to confide in her made her heart skip a beat. That had to mean something, right? She laid her head on his chest and hugged him hard.

"What's this for?" he asked.

"Because I—" She stopped herself when she realized the words that had almost spilled out of her mouth.

Because I love you.

Whoa.

Did she? Did she really love him, or was she just enormously infatuated? Was it possible to fall in love with someone in two weeks?

Daniel tipped her chin up to look at her. "Syd?"

"Just…because."

He must have seen through her, but she didn't give him a chance to question it. She slid her hands up his chest and behind his neck, and kissed him. The kind of kiss that she hoped would make him forget whatever it was he'd been about to say.

The low growl as he wound his fingers into her hair told her it was working. And she got so into it, she nearly forgot they were in a public place. When they broke apart, they were both a little breathless.

"You're getting me all frisky," he said.

"I want you frisky."

He grinned. "Lacey is sleeping over at Veronica's?"

"Yep."

"So you don't have to rush home?"

"Nope." She didn't have to be home at all. She'd told Lacey to call her cell if she needed anything, or if she decided to come home for any reason.

He flashed her a steamy smile. "Want to go to my place and make out?"

"Yes." Last night had been so...*fun*. It was almost like being a teenager again. Passionate necking and petting over the clothes. Although some skin-to-skin action would be nice, too. Why did he think she'd worn a skirt tonight?

"Maybe we should go soon. Just in case there's traffic or something."

"We probably should," he agreed, leaning down to nibble her earlobe. Then he cupped her behind and her legs went weak. "In fact, I think we should go right now."

NO ONE HAD EVER kissed Sydney as passionately, as *thoroughly,* as Daniel did. She couldn't get enough of his mouth. The feel of it and the taste of it.

She straddled him on the couch, knowing that as wonderful as kissing him was, this time it wasn't going to be enough. She was ready for more.

She wasn't just ready. She *needed* it. Maybe taking things slow had been a good idea two days ago, but everything was different now. Sometime over the past week and a half, she had stopped being afraid.

Daniel, on the other hand, didn't seem to be in a hurry. He was still holding back from taking that next step, so she took it for him.

She pulled her top up over her head and dropped it on the floor, and the rumbling sound Daniel made in his chest said he wasn't going to stop her. He wrapped his hands around her sides, running them upward, over her rib cage to hold her breasts, using his thumbs to tease her through the lace cups. She moaned and closed her eyes, convinced that every time he touched her it felt better and better.

"Your breasts are so beautiful," he said. He kissed the swell of one, then the other, and though it was pure bliss, it wasn't enough. She reached behind her to unfasten her bra, then tossed it on the floor.

"Even better," he said. He seemed content to just look for a while, but she wanted to be touched. She hooked a hand behind his neck and pulled him to her breast, and just before he took her nipple in his mouth, she could swear he mumbled something in Spanish, but it was drowned out by the sound of her own moans.

"Did you just speak Spanish?"

"Yes," he said, kissing his way to her other breast. She moaned and arched as he took that one in his mouth, too.

"What did you say?"

He gazed up at her and grinned. "You don't want to know."

"Yes, I do."

"It was a curse word. And not a very nice one."

"Can you say anything else?"

"A few words," he said, doing amazing things to her with his mouth. "Mostly I just know how to swear."

"Do you know how to say that you want to make love?"

"No, but…" He trailed off as the meaning of her question sank in, and his gaze shot up to hers. "Do you mean…?"

"Yes, I do. I want to make love."

"Are you sure?"

"I don't think I've ever been so sure of anything in my life." All of her apprehension, all of her fears, were just gone, as if they'd never even been there.

And her certainty must have shown in her face, because he didn't question her. "Bedroom?" he asked, but she shook her head.

"Here, like this." She fisted his shirt and tugged it over his head, but when she tried to get at his fly, her skirt got in the way.

"Take it off," he said, lifting her off his lap, and in the time it took to yank her skirt and panties down, his jeans and boxers were on the floor. And he was… perfect. Beautiful all over.

He sat up and tugged her closer, leaning in to press a kiss to her stomach, then another. He started working his way down, and when his tongue darted out to taste her, her legs nearly buckled. It felt so good, she didn't want him to stop, but she was so close already. This time when it happened, she wanted him inside her.

She pushed him back against the cushions and climbed over him, straddling his legs, trembling with anticipation. She centered herself over him and sank slowly down, taking him in. He gasped and dug his fingers into her hips. She rose up and sank back down.

Again and again. And it was so perfect she wanted to weep. This was how it was supposed to feel. This was what making love was supposed to be. And she did love him. She could feel it deep in her soul.

"Syd…" Daniel rasped. She wrapped her arms around his neck, feeling her muscles begin to tighten. Daniel cursed again, in English this time, and for some reason that pushed her over the edge. Pleasure gripped her like a vise, fast and hard, and when he groaned and rocked against her, she knew she'd taken him over with her.

She went limp against him and Daniel dropped his head on her shoulder, breathing hard.

"Tell me we didn't just have unprotected sex."

She sat back to look at him. "Of course not. I'm on the pill."

He blew out a relieved breath and let his head fall back against the cushions. "Thank God."

"I guess I should have mentioned that earlier."

"Yeah, because I think I just lost ten years off my life. I figured since you weren't sexually active, there was no reason for you to be on it."

"I take them to regulate my cycle."

"Good to know. And in case you're wondering, I got tested recently. I'm disease-free."

Which she should have considered before they made love. She'd just been so…swept away. She wasn't normally so irresponsible. In fact, Jeff's promiscuity was what had motivated her decision to stop sleeping with him.

"I hope I didn't ruin it for you," she said.

"Oh, no, not at all," he said. "I was so turned on

watching you that it took me a minute to realize I'd even forgotten. And for the record, I usually last longer than forty-five seconds."

"You know what's really cool?" she asked him.

"What?"

"You get to spend all night proving it to me."

CHAPTER THIRTEEN

"WHAT THE HECK are you doing?" Sydney asked Lacey, who was sitting on her bed sulking instead of packing. "We're leaving in less than an hour."

"I won't go," she said, folding her arms defiantly.

"It's only two days and we could both use a vacation."

"I'll stay home by myself," Lacey insisted. "I'm old enough."

"Nice try. You're coming with us, unless of course you want to stay with your dad and the bim...Kimberly."

Lacey narrowed her eyes. "I'd rather poke my eyes out with a fork."

"Then I guess you're coming with us."

Lacey got up and stomped her foot, something she hadn't done since she was six. "I want to stay here!"

"And people in Hell want ice water. Be ready, *or else.*"

"This sucks," Lacey shouted after her as Sydney returned to her bedroom to pack the last of her things. She had no idea why Lacey was so against going to Jason's. Especially since Angie's son, Jordan, would be there. What teenage girl wouldn't want to hang out at the ocean on the beach for two days sunning herself with a cute boy?

And Sydney had seen him. He was really cute.

At Lacey's age, Sydney would have been thrilled. Of course, growing up in Michigan, they didn't exactly have access to the ocean. Lots of lakes, though. Not that her mother had ever taken her to one. Maybe when she was little, when her father was still around. She honestly didn't remember. It was the reason she had always tried to do those sorts of things with Lacey. Why she figured Lacey would enjoy this trip.

So much for *that* brilliant plan.

April was in her bouncy seat on Sydney's bedroom floor and she squealed happily when Sydney walked back in. "At least you're happy to see me," she mumbled, opening her lingerie drawer. She paused when she realized her silk camisole wasn't there.

"Lacey!" she called and Lacey stuck her head in the bedroom door a second later, scowling. "What."

"Did you borrow my white silk camisole?"

"No."

"Have you seen it anywhere? Did it maybe get mixed in with your clothes?"

She huffed. "*No.* You probably left it at Daniel's house."

Sydney shot her daughter a warning look.

"*What?* I'm just sayin'."

Even if she'd been trying to hide their relationship from Lacey, they had blown that when she'd walked in on them kissing in the kitchen the other day. Sydney thought she might be upset, but all Lacey did was say, "Ew, Mom, get a room," and go back to her bedroom.

The truth is, it was a small miracle that Lacey hadn't

seen anything earlier. Ever since Saturday night when she and Daniel had made love, Sydney hadn't been able to keep her hands off him. It was embarrassing, really, how completely under his spell she had slipped. Maybe it was hormonal, or her body was making up for lost time, but she couldn't seem to get enough of him. They made love in the evenings after April went to bed, and she'd started coming over an hour early in the mornings, after Lacey went to work, waking Daniel in some very creative ways. She'd even started scheduling April's nap when she knew he would be on break and stopping by the house. It was amazing what they could accomplish in fifteen minutes when properly motivated.

She'd begun to worry that she might wear the poor guy out, but so far he hadn't complained. The fact that she'd been so nervous about not being able to please him now seemed utterly ridiculous.

And while she had spent a lot of time naked at Daniel's house, she always wore her undergarments home.

"I did not leave it at Daniel's," she told Lacey.

Lacey shrugged. *"Whatever,"* she said on her way to her room. She was back a few minutes later, the camisole in her hand, looking a little less cocky. "I guess it did get stuck in my laundry."

When Sydney was finished packing she carried her suitcase and April to the kitchen. She heard raised voices out the side door and looked out. Daniel and Angie were standing in the driveway, by the rear of Sydney's van, arguing.

"This is not my fault!" Angie was saying.

"Well, if they don't have to go, I shouldn't have to go," Daniel said.

"Come on, Danny. Don't be like that."

Uh-oh. Maybe she'd just strong-armed Lacey into packing for no reason.

Leaving April securely in her seat, Sydney stepped outside. Daniel and his sister appeared to be at a stand-off, and Angie was obviously on the verge of tears.

"Sydney," Angie said, clearly relieved to see her. "Would you please talk some sense into him?"

"What's going on?" she asked.

"He's being a jerk, that's what!"

Daniel turned to her. "Dee's boyfriend dumped her. So she isn't going. And now Beth isn't going because she doesn't want to leave Dee alone. And the *only* reason I agreed to go is because *they* were going."

And Sydney could see he was pretty dead set against going. He was going to need some serious incentive.

"Angie, could you excuse us a minute?" Sydney said, and gestured Daniel into the house. When they were inside she said, "Why don't you want to go?"

"Look, it's no secret that I don't like Jason. I didn't want to go on this trip, but Angie guilted me into it. She made it sound like some big family thing because Beth and Dee were going to be there. But if they don't have to go, I don't think I should have to, either."

"It obviously means a lot to Angie."

"She'll get over it."

"You don't care that you're hurting her feelings? She's almost in tears. She doesn't strike me as the type to cry unless she's really upset."

Daniel frowned and folded his arms across his chest.

"You can make an exception, just this once."

"Once? I'm *constantly* humoring her."

Sydney doubted that. "Then do it for me," she said, unfolding his arms and stepping into them, pressing against him in a way that she knew would drive him crazy. "Think how much fun we could have."

His arms closed around her and something warm and sexy sparked in his eyes. "What did you have in mind?"

"I think we could get creative. And fewer people there means more time alone."

She could see she was getting to him. "Keep talking."

"I've really been looking forward to this," she said, rising up on her toes to give his lips a soft nibble. "Pretty please?"

"Ugh, gross." Lacey said from behind them. Sydney turned to see her standing in the kitchen doorway, her stuffed duffel bag on the floor beside her. "So, are we going or not?"

She had obviously heard at least part of the discussion. Sydney looked up at Daniel. "Are we going?"

He sighed and shook his head, as if he couldn't believe what he was about to say. "Yes, we're going."

"Dude," Lacey said, shaking her head sadly, "you are so whipped."

"Go put your duffel in the van," Sydney told her. "And strap April into her car seat."

Lacey plucked April out of her bouncy seat and headed outside.

"She's right," Daniel said. "You owe me big-time."

It was a debt she looked forward to paying in full.

ANGIE LEANED FORWARD and whispered to Sydney from the middle bench seat where she sat with April. "What's with those two?"

Sydney looked to the back of the van, where Lacey sat hunched into the corner next to the window, her black lipstick intensifying the scowl she'd been wearing since they left, iPod blaring. Jordan occupied the opposite end, the brim of his baseball cap pulled down over his eyes, arms folded over his chest, his music equally loud.

"I don't know," she whispered back, although she doubted they could hear her. They probably wouldn't hear a nuclear explosion. "Do they not like each other?"

Angie shrugged. "I have no idea. They work together every day and Jordan hasn't mentioned them not getting along. Of course, Jordan doesn't say much about anything. He had a girlfriend for three months before I heard a word about it."

"Of course they like each other," Daniel said from the driver's seat, not even bothering to lower his voice. "That's why they're acting like they don't. I don't even have kids and I know that."

"Maybe if they were twelve," Sydney said.

"She's right," Angie told him. "Kids their age should've grown out of that."

Daniel shrugged. "Whatever you say."

Angie gave his shoulder a playful shove. "Trust us on this. We're mothers, we know our kids."

They passed the sign marking their arrival to Stillwater.

"Where to now?" Daniel asked.

"Follow this road through the city," Angie said. "Jason's place is south of town."

Daniel drove through the congested streets of what looked like a trendy tourist town, until they reached the cove. Though it was nearly eight o'clock, people still occupied a long expanse of white, sandy, private beach. An assortment of canoes and sailboats dotted the clear blue water. The only thing bluer than the water was the pallet of cloudless sky. They couldn't have asked for a more perfect day to begin their vacation.

Reaching the end of town, they followed the road south, driving parallel to the shoreline for several minutes then turned off on a narrow residential road.

"It's the last house on the right," Angie said. They passed several mid-size homes and a row of luxury condos, but when Sydney saw the sprawling white, Cape Cod-style home set off by itself at the end of the road, her jaw nearly landed in her lap.

"This is a *vacation* home?" Sydney asked.

"I know. Isn't it beautiful? It belongs to Jason's parents. It's been in their family since before Jason was born."

"How big is it?"

"Thirty-five hundred square feet. Six bedrooms, three baths. And what I love is that they don't have a single television in the house."

Daniel glanced in the rearview mirror at the kids. "That should go over really well."

He pulled up the long dirt drive and around to the front of the house, pulling up in front of a porch that spanned the entire length of the house. Beyond the house the landscape dipped to a wide strip of private beach with a breathtaking view of the entire cove.

The door opened and a tall, slender man, who Sydney assumed was Jason, stepped out on the porch. Angie's eyes lit up and she hopped out of the van. Jason's smile said he was just as happy to see her. They met at the bottom of the porch steps and Angie launched herself in his arms. They were clearly crazy about each other, which didn't seem to go over well with Daniel, if the scowl he wore was any indication. Sydney hoped he would at least be civilized.

"I'll get April," he grumbled, and Sydney got out to stretch her legs, breathing in the salty ocean air.

Jordan and Lacey climbed out as Angie and Jason walked over to the van.

"Hey, Jason," Jordan said, speaking for the first time since they'd left the house. Jason greeted him with some complicated handshake and Jordan actually smiled. "Not bad."

"Told you I would get it," Jason said.

"Sydney, this is Jason," Angie said, practically glowing she looked so happy.

"Sydney," he said with a warm smile, reaching out to shake her hand. "It's wonderful to finally meet you."

He was very attractive, but older than Sydney expected, or maybe it was the salt-and-pepper hair aging him. "You, too. You have a beautiful home."

"And this is Lacey," Angie told him.

If Jason was shocked by her appearance, he didn't let it show. "Hi, Lacey. Nice to meet you. I have twin daughters who are right around your age. Fifteen, right?"

Lacey nodded. "Are they here?"

"Unfortunately not. They live in Los Angeles with their mom. We'll have to all get together some time when they're visiting."

Lacey nodded. "Cool."

Daniel emerged from the van holding April.

"Hey, Daniel," Jason said.

Daniel politely shook his hand, but there was obvious tension between them.

"And this must be April," Jason said, taking her sticky fist and shaking it, too, which made her gurgle excitedly in Daniel's arms. "She's a cutie. It seems like yesterday mine were this small."

He seemed so nice, Sydney couldn't help wondering what Daniel didn't like about him. It was clear from in the way Jason looked at Angie that he adored her.

"I wasn't sure if anyone would be hungry so I took some hot dogs out," Jason said. "I thought we could build a bonfire."

Sydney hadn't roasted hotdogs over a fire since summer camp when she was eight.

"That sounds like fun," Angie said, smiling up at him.

"Can I help with the bags?" he asked Daniel.

"Sure," Daniel said, handing April to Sydney.

Angie looped one arm through Sydney's and the other through Lacey's, who surprisingly didn't object. "Come on, I'll give you guys a tour of the house."

Though it was enormous, the house had a distinctly cozy and lived-in feel. Decorated in a mishmash of furniture styles from a dozen different eras, it possessed a slightly jumbled but appealing quality. Comfortable, yet functional. Just what she would expect from a summer home.

"This is really nice," Sydney told her.

"I'll show you where you'll be sleeping," Angie said leading them up a slightly creaky staircase to the second level.

"Only the master on the main floor has its own bath, so everyone up here will have to share." She gestured into a bedroom the was distinctly feminine and told Lacey, "This will be your room. It's where the girls usually stay. Sydney, you and Daniel have the bedroom at the end of the hall."

Her and Daniel? "Daniel and I are sharing a room?"

Angie blinked. "Yeah, I thought…"

They were sleeping together? Yeah, but not with her daughter down the hall.

Lacey, however, seemed to know exactly what was going on. "Mom, it's okay," she said. "I don't care if you guys share a room."

"Lacey—"

"You think I don't know what goes on at Daniel's house every night?"

Naively, she had hoped not. If her own mother had

shared a room with a man after the divorce, Sydney would have been horrified. Of course, her mom hadn't been stable enough to date. Most days, she didn't even get out of bed.

But Sydney didn't want Lacey to feel she had to accept it if it made her uncomfortable. "Honey, are you positive it's okay? Because I won't be upset if it's not."

"It's totally cool," Lacey said. "I'm gonna go down and grab my bag."

"I'm really sorry about that," Angie said when she was back downstairs. "I wasn't thinking."

"It's okay."

"She's a great kid."

Sydney smiled. "She definitely has her moments."

Angie showed her to the room she and Daniel would be sharing. It was small but cozy, with antique furniture and French doors that led to a balcony overlooking the ocean. There was even an old portable crib with a mobile set up in the corner for April.

"This is beautiful," Sydney told her. She laid April in the crib and the baby squealed excitedly when she saw the mobile, kicking her legs, before rolling over onto her belly and pushing herself up on her arms.

"Hey! Look at that," Angie said.

"She started doing that last week. You should have seen how excited Daniel was the first time he saw her. You would have thought she was the first baby in history to roll over by herself."

Angie crouched down beside the crib. "He seems to love her. It's hard to imagine that he could give her up at this point."

"I know." But as far as Sydney knew he was still looking for April's family. What she really hoped was that someday she and Lacey and Daniel and April could be a family. But she knew it would be a long time before he was ready for that. She could wait. This time, she was determined not to rush things.

"So what did you think of Jason?" Angie asked, pulling herself to her feet.

"He seems really nice. And it's obvious he's crazy about you."

"I've been divorced for seventeen years and Jason is the first man I've ever seriously considered spending the rest of my life with. The truth is, I've always been kind of a jerk magnet. And Danny knows that. But Jason is different. He's...*amazing*. I just wish Danny could see it."

"I'm sure he will once he gets to know him."

"I hope this weekend wasn't a bad idea. Oh, by the way." She gave Sydney a quick, firm hug. "Thank you for talking him into coming. I don't know what you had to promise him as leverage, but I hope it isn't too much of a hardship."

Sydney couldn't fight the smile curling her lips. "Oh, it won't be."

Angie laughed. "Why do I get the feeling that if I'd put you in separate rooms, you would have wound up together anyway?"

"What's this about separate rooms?" Daniel asked, appearing in the doorway with their luggage.

"I was just saying," Angie started, then she looked

from Daniel to Sydney and shook her head. "Never mind. I'm going to go find Jason."

When she was gone Daniel set the bags on the floor by the closet and said, "So, we're sharing a room?"

"If that's okay."

"You know it's okay with me, but how will Lacey feel about it?"

She loved that he cared enough to worry about her daughter's feelings. "She says she's fine with it."

"Good." A sly smile lifted the corners of his mouth as he shut the bedroom door. "I've been looking forward to spending the night with you again."

"Me, too." They'd only spent the night together that one time, but it had been so nice sleeping curled up against him and waking in his arms.

He started toward her, giving her the look he usually had just before their clothes started flying. "So, what do you want to do?"

She stopped him with a hand on his chest. "I think we're supposed to be downstairs for a bonfire."

He sighed and flopped down on the bed, which made a loud creak. "No way," he said, bouncing a few times. The bed groaned under his weight. "Is this a cruel joke?"

"It is a little loud. I'm sure we can figure something out."

There was a soft knock at the door and Daniel got up to open it. Lacey stood on the other side, looking wary, as if she was afraid she might see something gross. "Angie said to tell you to come downstairs. They're starting the fire. And she said bring a sweater because it gets chilly after dark."

"Tell her we'll be right down. I just have to change April," Sydney said.

Lacey left and Sydney scooped April out of the play-pen and laid her on the bed to change her.

"By the way," Daniel said, "when we were bringing the bags in I asked Jordan what the deal was with him and Lacey."

"What did he say?"

"He shrugged and said, 'Nothing.'"

"So they *don't* like each other."

"No, that means they *do*."

She frowned. "That makes no sense."

"It makes perfect sense."

"And you're the relationship expert?"

He just smiled. "You'll see."

SYDNEY WAS *SO* GONNA GET IT when Daniel got her upstairs.

They'd spend the last hour and a half cuddled up together on a lounge chair under a blanket by the fire, and she'd had a severe case of wandering hands. Every time he'd let his guard down one would be trailing up his thigh or sneaking under his sweatshirt. He sat there in a constant state of semiarousal, counting the minutes until they could be alone. If he'd thought to bring his handcuffs, he could have resolved the issue by locking her to the chair. Which evoked some very interesting scenarios, making the problem worse.

By eleven-thirty Daniel was in agony. He made a production out of yawning and said, "I'm beat."

"It is getting late," Angie said. "Maybe we should call it a night."

Sydney couldn't get off his lap fast enough. She must have been as eager to go upstairs as he was, but like him, she probably hadn't wanted to be rude.

"I'll go put April to bed," Sydney said, and lifted April from her bouncy seat, where she'd been sleeping soundly since ten.

Daniel hung back to help douse the fire, then he, Jordan and Jason carried the chairs back up to the porch, while Lacey and Angie brought in the hot chocolate cups and sticky marshmallow skewers.

When everything was cleaned up, and all the doors locked, he said good-night and headed upstairs. The bedroom door was closed, so he knocked softly.

"Come in," she said in a loud whisper. He opened the door to find the room dark and Sydney already in bed. He reached to turn on a lamp but she whispered, "Don't. You might wake her. She's restless."

He closed the door as quietly as possible and tiptoed to the side of the bed. "Are you naked under there?"

She smiled and lifted up the covers. Oh, yeah.

He shed his clothes and climbed in beside her, wincing as the bed creaked under his weight. "Man, that's loud."

"Then we'll just have to do something that doesn't require a lot of movement," Sydney said with a smile that said she already had something in mind. She carefully sat up, trying to make the least noise possible, and threw a leg over him, straddling his thighs. He was about to ask how she thought this would be a quieter alternative, but then she kissed him. His mouth, his chin, the side of his neck. Then she started working her way lower. Down his chest, then his stomach, until it was clear where she was going with this.

She circled her hand around his erection, leaning over, and he felt the heat her breath…then April started to cry.

He cursed.

"I'll try propping her bottle up," Sydney said, crawling off the bed and walking to the crib, trying to get April to settle down, while he lay there in agony. After a minute April quieted, and Sydney crept back to the bed, but the second she leaned on the mattress, and it creaked, the baby jolted awake again.

Sydney sighed and sagged in defeat. "Why do I get the feeling she's not going to let us have any fun."

"She's in a strange place, in an unfamiliar bed. I guess we should have expected this." Daniel grabbed his boxers from the floor and pulled them on. April wasn't in full-blown hysterics yet, but if he let it go that far she would wake the whole house. "Give her to me."

Sydney lifted the baby out of the crib and handed her to Daniel.

"Hey, munchkin," he said, stretching out on his side and laying her down beside him, with her back to his chest and she calmed right down. He had the feeling he would be pretty much stuck like this for the rest of the night.

Sydney slipped into a pair of panties and a T-shirt and

climbed into bed, lying on her side facing him. "Maybe tomorrow?"

He reached over and took her hand. "I'm sure we can work something out."

"Besides, it's not like we didn't already make love this morning."

"Twice." And every day for the past week. Maybe they were getting spoiled.

"I had a lot of fun tonight," she said.

"Groping me?"

She smiled. "That, too. But I meant in general. Just hanging out with Angie and Jason. He's a great guy."

"Hmm."

"I don't understand why you don't like him. You should at least try for Angie's sake. She's crazy about him."

"I don't trust him. He's *too* nice. Just like Richard. If you could have seen how messed up she was—"

"That was a *long* time ago. And the fact that she hasn't had a serious relationship since the divorce is a pretty good sign that she's not going to fall for just anyone."

Sydney had a point, but every one of Daniel's instincts was telling him that he needed to protect his sister. So that was what he planned to do.

CHAPTER FOURTEEN

THOUGH LACEY HAD PLANNED to have a terrible time all weekend to spite her mom, and she was still kinda pissed that she'd been forced here in the first place, it really hadn't been that bad. Mostly because Jordan was doing everything he could to avoid her.

It had been like that at work lately, too. He would bark occasional orders, but otherwise he ignored her, and she ignored him right back. She could hardly believe that she'd thought she liked him. He was the biggest jerk she had ever met. Even worse than Shane.

Everyone got up late Saturday morning, and after a huge breakfast of eggs, bacon and homemade waffles, the adults got dressed and went for a tour around the cove on Jason's boat. Lacey stayed at the house to babysit April and was relieved when Jordan took off jogging down the beach. She didn't like the idea of being stuck alone with him.

She played with April on a blanket in the sand for a while, then gave her a bottle and put her down for a nap. It was weird, but she had half expected to see creepy Fred out there. It seemed as though he was hanging around everywhere she went, spreading his creepiness. When she was picking up trash off the strip mall grass the other day before the mowers went through, she'd seen him hanging out in front of the pub across the street. And when she and Veronica went to get ice cream the other night, he was in line behind them.

He never said anything to her, or even looked at her. She was sure it was just a coincidence, but still it gave her the creeps.

Since she hadn't taken one that morning, she grabbed a quick shower while April was asleep. Thinking she was still alone in the house, she dried off and wrapped herself in a towel, grabbed her dirty clothes and started down the hall to her room...running face-first into Jordan, who was standing just outside the door.

He was shirtless and sweaty. And so gorgeous she had to remind herself again how much she didn't like him.

"Took you long enough," he said.

She glared up at him, clutching the towel to her chest. "Has anyone ever told you you're a Neanderthal?"

He looked down at her and without warning a lop-sided grin spread across his face. It was the first time he'd ever smiled at her, and for a second it actually took her breath away.

He reached out and touched a damp lock of her hair. She had to fight not to flinch. "It's not green anymore."

"It's a gel—it washed out."

His eyes wandered across her face, in the same slow, precise way he did everything, and she started to feel nervous.

"What are you looking at?"

"You're pretty without all of that garbage on your face."

Garbage on her face? She suddenly remembered who she was talking to and shoved him away. "You're a jerk."

He let out a surprised laugh. "I compliment you and you call me a jerk?"

"I'm pretty without the *garbage* on my face. You call *that* a compliment? You don't even like me. You're just messing with my head again."

"Again? When did I ever mess with your head?"

"When you helped me get rid of Shane. You made me believe you liked me."

His brow lifted, and she realized how that had sounded.

Good going, Lacey. She'd just let him know he'd gotten to her, that she *wanted* him to like her. She tried to push past him but he stepped in front of her.

"Why does it matter if I like you or not?"

"It doesn't. Now get out of my way." She tried to get past him again, but he wrapped a large sweaty hand around her forearm. He wasn't even kissing her this time, and she was getting those funny feelings again. *All* over.

"I don't understand why you do this," he said.

"Do what?"

"This." Jordan reached up his other hand and brushed his finger over the ring piercing her brow. Every inch of her tingled with awareness. "The piercings, the dark makeup. And why do you change your hair weird colors?

Why do you do all of this…*garbage* when you look so pretty without it?"

He thought she was pretty? She hated that the idea made her heart beat faster. Why did she care what he thought? He was a creep.

"To be different," she said.

"Why do you want to be different?"

At first she thought he was being a jerk again, but when she looked into his eyes she could see he genuinely didn't understand. And for some reason that made her uncomfortable. She lowered her gaze and shrugged. "I don't know, I just do."

"There has to be a reason." He let go of her arm and lifted her chin until their eyes met. His expression was so intense she almost couldn't stand it. She wasn't used to anyone looking at her that way, as if he could see right through her. People stared all the time, but they never really *saw* her. And that was exactly the way she liked it. They hit the surface and bounced off.

"I guess I want people to notice me."

Jordan's mouth curled up in a grin that made her stomach plummet. "Trust me, people would notice you anyway."

He ran his thumb over her bottom lip and her heart started slam dancing with her ribs.

She turned her head. "Don't do that."

"Why? I like your lip. It always sticks out, like you're pouting."

She caught her lip in her teeth. "I should go check on April."

"Already did. She's asleep." He dipped his head,

so their mouths were almost touching. She could feel his breath, feel the heat radiating from his body like a furnace.

"Are you going to kiss me?" she asked, but the words came out all soft and breathy.

"Do you always ask first?"

"I don't like surprises."

"Maybe I will. But you have to promise me something first."

Lacey's heart was beating so hard and fast she felt light-headed. "What?"

"No more weird hair color or crazy makeup."

All those warm, trembly feelings fizzled away. Just when she thought he was a nice guy, he had to go and *ruin* it.

"Drop dead," she said, shoving him away. "If you can't accept me for who really I am, I would rather remove my own skin with a vegetable peeler than kiss you."

Jordan shook his head, giving her that blank look again. God, she *hated* that.

"As soon as you figure out who that is, you let me know." With that, he walked past her into the bathroom, and shut the door behind him. She hated to admit it, but the words stung.

When April began to cry several minutes later, Lacey was still standing there.

SOMETHING WAS UP.

Jason and Angie disappeared into the master suite for about an hour that afternoon. At the time, Sydney figured they were doing what any couple would do when locked in a bedroom—what she wished she and Daniel could do—but when they emerged to make dinner, something was off. Angie seemed nervous. Jason kept looking at her and smiling, and Angie kept looking from Daniel to Jordan, then back to Jason, as if she was waiting for something. Or waiting for the right time to say something.

And Sydney had the sneaking suspicion that whatever it was, Angie was pretty sure Daniel and Jordan weren't going to like it. Which made Sydney nervous. They'd had a good time so far. She hated to see it ruined.

After dinner, everyone pitched in and helped clean up, and when they were finished, Angie said, "Why don't we all sit on the porch. Jason and I have something we need to talk to you about."

Daniel shot a look Sydney's way, as if he thought she knew what was going on, and she shrugged. Everyone seemed puzzled as they walked out onto the porch.

It was a gorgeous evening. The sun was just beginning to set over the water, reflecting the reddish-orange streaks that spread across the darkening sky.

Sydney and Daniel sat on the swing with April while Jordan and Lacey took chairs on opposite sides of the porch. Angie and Jason leaned against the railing with their backs to the sunset. He took her hand and gave it a squeeze.

Angie cut right to the chase. "Jason and I are getting married."

Sydney felt Daniel tense beside her.

"That's great," Jordan said, looking genuinely happy

for his mom. "But I thought you were going to wait until next year."

"We were," Angie said.

"So why don't you?" Daniel asked, in a tone that made his sister flinch.

"Because," Jason said, "Angie and I are having a baby."

"Wow," Jordan said, looking stunned. "I didn't know you were planning on having kids."

"We weren't," Angie said, glancing at her brother. "This was a big surprise. But now that the shock has worn off, we're both excited."

"When did you find out?" Jordan asked.

"I took the test before dinner. Two tests, actually, just to be sure."

"Excuse me," Daniel mumbled, pushing off the swing with such force Sydney jerked forward and almost lost her grip on April. He walked into the house, letting the screen door bang shut behind him.

Angie's face fell, and any trace of joy and excitement disappeared. Though Sydney could tell he was trying to hide it, Jason was clearly angry. "Do you want me to talk to him?" he asked.

Angie shook her head, looking miserable. "It will only make things worse. I guess it was too much to expect him to be happy for me."

Jordan got up, and gave his mom a kiss on the cheek and a big hug. "*I'm* happy for you."

"So am I," Sydney said, and Lacey added, "Me, too."

Angie smiled and wiped away the tear that had

escaped down her cheek. "Thanks, everyone. That really means a lot to me."

"I'm going to go talk to Daniel," Sydney said, rising from the swing. Someone had to tell him what a jerk he was being. And maybe Angie thought Sydney might be able to reason with him because she didn't try to stop her.

She passed April to Lacey, then went inside to look for him. But he wasn't on the main floor. He wasn't in the bedroom, either. She checked the entire house, but there was no sign of him anywhere. He must have slipped out the back and gone for a walk. And since she had no idea which direction he had taken, she couldn't go after him.

All she could do was wait.

THE WAY JORDAN HUGGED and kissed his mom...well, that was really sweet. Maybe he wasn't as big a jerk as Lacey had thought.

After everyone else went inside, he walked down to the beach by himself. Lacey gave him a few minutes, then followed him. He was sitting in the sand, close to the shore, looking out over the water.

She sat down beside him, propping her arms on her raised knees, wondering if he might tell her to get lost. He glanced over at her, but didn't say anything.

"That was awesome," she said. "The way you hugged your mom."

He shrugged, as if it was no big deal. "She looked like she needed it."

"Daniel was acting like a tool."

"Yeah. He's just really protective of her because of my dad."

"He didn't like your dad, either?"

"I guess he used to, until he found out that my dad was beating the crap out of her."

Lacey sucked in a surprised breath. She never would have guessed that someone like Angie would let anyone hit her. And she couldn't understand why someone would want to. And she was even more astonished that Jordan had told her.

"Did you ever see him do it?" she asked.

"No, they got divorced when I was a baby. I found out about it when I was ten, when he went to jail for doing the same thing to his second wife. I was supposed to visit him in Washington for two weeks during summer vacation. My mom felt I had the right to know why I couldn't go."

"How long was he in jail?"

"Just a couple of months. But all his visitation rights were revoked. He had to go to therapy for a long time before they would let me see him again. And then he had to come to California. I wasn't allowed to go back to Washington until I was fifteen."

"My dad cheated on my mom," Lacey said. She didn't mean to. It just sort of came out.

"Is that why they got divorced?"

She nodded. "And I think she knew about it for a long time before she left him. Everyone did. It was humiliating."

"Parents do really stupid things sometimes."

They were quiet for a minute, then she said, "Can I ask you a question?"

"I guess."

"Why were you such a jerk to me at work?"

"When you came to the office that first day I figured you were a spoiled private school girl," he said, then a smile tipped up the side of his mouth. "Yet, as much as I didn't like you, I was somehow strangely attracted to you."

She smiled. "Me, too."

"Yeah. I figured as much."

"You know, you were right. This isn't really me. All this *garbage*. I only do it to piss my dad off."

"Yeah, I figured that, too."

"It was worth it for a while, knowing how much he hated it. Honestly, now I'm just getting sick of it. But I know if I go back to the way I looked before, he'll be really happy, and I don't want to give him the satisfaction."

"Maybe it's time to stop worrying about what *he* wants, and do what *you* want."

He was right.

Lacey reached up and unhooked her brow ring, pulled it out and flung it at the water. Moonlight glinted off its surface then it disappeared beneath the surface.

"Better?" he asked.

Better, but not enough. She pushed herself up onto her feet, kicked off her flip-flops, and walked to the edge of water. She paused for a second, then stepped into the surf, clothes and all, and waded out a ways. Then she took a deep breath and dove under. She swam a few feet, washing the gel from her hair. When she broke the surface and scrubbed her hands over her face, the salty sea water stung her eyes. But it was a good sting.

She walked back to the shore, where Jordan stood watching her. Her clothes were wet and heavy and she was freezing, but she felt a million times better.

"How's that?" she asked, smiling up at him.

Jordan didn't say a word. He just smiled, wrapped his arms around her and kissed her.

AFTER SEEING the hurt look on Angie's face as he stormed off the porch, Daniel knew immediately that he was being an ass. But he couldn't seem to make himself go back and apologize. Not until he'd had a chance to think things through. Which was what he had been doing for the past couple of hours as he paced up and down the shore.

And as he walked, he began to realize that he'd been so worried Angie would get hurt again and so suspicious of Jason's motives that he'd been blind to fact that the only person hurting her now was him.

The truth was, Jason had never said or done anything to suggest he wasn't genuinely devoted to Angie. Daniel had tried and convicted the guy before he ever had a chance. Guilty until proven innocent.

And Daniel had to wonder if part of the reason he didn't like Jason was simple jealousy. Daniel had been Angie's protector for a long time, and though he complained, maybe he wasn't ready to pass the torch.

Maybe the thought of losing her to Jason permanently was too much to take on the heels of the news he'd gotten

from the P.I. yesterday. The investigator had a good lead
on a cousin of Reanne's and needed the okay to fly out
to Utah to look into it. A month ago, Daniel wouldn't
have hesitated to write him out a check. He didn't want
to keep April. And even if he did, he couldn't give her
what she needed—two parents and a stable home.

None of that was part of Daniel's plan. He didn't
want to be permanently tied down to anyone. Yet when
he tried to imagine Sydney and April not being there
to greet him when he got home from work, when he
thought of Sydney not crawling into bed with him every
morning before he started his day, he felt so…empty.

He tried to tell himself that it was habit. He'd seen
so much of her lately, he'd probably gotten used to her
being around. Meaning he could just as easily get un-
used to her, too. At some point he was going to have to
back off. Maybe if he let the relationship run its natural
course, he wouldn't have to worry about anyone's heart
breaking. Maybe they could end this as friends.

But what if it wasn't so easy to let go this time?
Which would he regret more? Making a commitment
to Sydney, or walking away from her for good?

The house was dark when he got back, and though he
wouldn't have blamed Angie and Jason if they'd locked
him out, the door was open. He climbed the stairs, careful not to wake anyone, and crept into the bedroom.
Sydney was curled up on her side, April tucked against
her. He'd been a real jerk to dump April on her like that,
knowing she would feel obligated to take care of her.
Proof that he would be a lousy father.

He undressed and got into bed as gently as possible, but the horrendous squeaking woke Sydney.

"Hey, you're back," she whispered sleepily. "I was worried."

He lay facing her. "I needed some time alone to think. I'm sorry I stomped off like that. I acted like a complete ass."

"Yeah, you did."

Her candid response made him smile. He liked that she didn't let him get away with anything.

He touched her cheek, smoothed a stray curl behind her ear. "I'm going to talk to them and make this right. If they ever speak to me again, that is."

"All Angie wants is for you to be happy for her."

"I am. Or at least, I'm trying to be."

"The fact that she loves Jason doesn't mean she loves you any less."

God, was he that transparent? "I know."

"Have you ever heard why Jason and his wife got divorced?"

"Angie never mentioned it." Probably because she knew he wouldn't listen. And didn't care.

"She left him for someone else. He said he was blind-sided. He didn't even have a clue she was having an affair, but it had been going on for over a year. He was devastated."

"Well, he won't have to worry about that with Angie. He'll never find a woman more devoted."

"Why do you think he loves her so much? He told me that she taught him to trust again."

Jason was always so confident and put-together, it

never occurred to Daniel that he might be just as vulnerable as Angie. That he had a lot to lose, too. And maybe Jason wasn't the only one with trust issues. When Angie married Richard, Daniel had welcomed him into the family without question. He had been like the brother Daniel never had. Daniel had trusted him to take care of Angie, and Richard had betrayed that trust in the worst way. He hoped he could learn to trust Jason.

He was about to tell Sydney that, but when he looked over, he realized she'd gone back to sleep.

DANIEL MANAGED to get a few hours of restless sleep, but he woke at five, guilt gnawing his insides. He rolled out of bed and dressed as quietly as he could and headed downstairs, surprised to smell coffee. It seemed he wasn't the only one who couldn't sleep.

There was no one in the kitchen, but the front door was open. He poured himself a cup of coffee and stepped out on the porch. Jason sat in one of the chairs, in his robe. He looked up as the storm door creaked open.

"You're awake early," Jason said. "I hope it's because you feel like a piece of crap for what you did to your sister."

Ouch. That was the first time Jason had been anything but perfectly polite to Daniel, even though Daniel had at times been less that warm and friendly. Apparently there was a limit to what Jason would take, and Daniel had found it.

"I do."

"You know," Jason said, looking out over the water, "I don't really give a damn what you think about me,

Daniel. You can be a jerk to me if that's what you want. I don't care. But you hurt the woman I love and that is not acceptable. And if you do it again…" He met Daniel's eye. "Badge or no badge, I *will* take you down."

Daniel didn't doubt that for a second. And it confirmed to him that Jason would never hurt Angie. It was time for Daniel to let her go.

"If it'll make you feel better, take a swing at me now. God knows I've earned it."

"Don't think I'm not tempted. You really hurt her. But Angie would have my head, because no matter how much of an ass you've been, she still loves you."

"It won't happen again."

Jason looked up at Daniel. Really studied him, then said, "I believe you."

He was cutting Daniel a hell of a lot more slack than Daniel had ever cut him.

"I also want to say congratulations. About the baby."

Jason smiled. "Thanks."

"I guess it must have really come as a shock."

"More for Angie than me. I always wanted more kids. And who knows, with twins running in both our families, we might even get two."

The thought of Angie juggling a career and newborn twins made Daniel smile.

"Hey," Jason said suddenly. "Do you fish?"

"Not since I was a kid."

"We should go."

"Now?"

"Why not?"

Fishing with Jason? Weirder things had happened. "Sure, I'll go fishing."

"Great. Why don't you go wake Jordan up. Meet me down at the boat in fifteen minutes."

"Sure." Daniel went upstairs to Jordan's room. He had just lifted his hand to knock, when across the hall Lacey's door creaked open and he caught a shirtless Jordan red-handed.

Jordan went beet-red when he saw Daniel standing there.

So much for them not liking each other.

"This isn't what it looks like," Jordan said.

Through the open door Daniel could see Lacey, still sleeping under the covers. What the hell was he supposed to say at a time like this?

"You want to go fishing?" he asked.

For a second Jordan looked confused, as if maybe it was a trick question. "Uh, sure."

"Jason said to meet him at the boat in fifteen minutes."

Now he looked downright baffled. "You're going fishing with *Jason?*"

"Yep."

"Did I miss something?"

Daniel just smiled. "Get ready."

Daniel peeked in on Sydney and April, who were both sound asleep, and grabbed his shoes and socks. Jordan was waiting for him by the door when he got downstairs.

"You ready?" Daniel asked.

"Uh, yeah," Jordan said, but hesitated. "Uncle Danny, you're not gonna tell my mom about me being in Lacey's room, are you?"

"Should I?"

"No! We were just talking."

"That's funny, the last time I *just talked* to a woman, I remember leaving my shirt on."

Jordan grinned sheepishly. "Okay, maybe that's not *all* we did."

"Be careful."

"I will."

"I don't know if you talk to your dad about stuff like this."

"Considering the circumstances, I don't talk to him about much of anything. But my mom has been drilling me on the virtues of safe sex since I was thirteen."

That sounded like Angie.

"Besides," he added, "Lacey wants to wait until she's married."

Daniel was genuinely surprised. He didn't think kids these days held out in the face of peer pressure. Of course, Lacey did seem to march to the beat of her own drummer. "And how do you feel about that?" he asked Jordan.

"I think it's kinda cool. And it's not about sex, anyway. I mean, I really like her that way, but I also like just being with her. Talking and stuff. She gets me. You know what I mean?"

He nodded. He knew exactly what Jordan meant. And he was proud of him. In a way, he wished he had a son he could talk to. Give advice to. Daniel used to be a pretty integral part of his nephew's life, but with Jason in the picture now, Jordan might not need him as much.

And that was okay, because it was obvious that Jordan liked and respected Jason.

He heard Jason start the boat. "We should probably go, before he leaves without us."

Jordan followed him down to the dock and onto the boat. Jason, wearing a John Deere cap and a pair of dark sunglasses, sat waiting in the captain's chair, a cigar clenched between his teeth. "Welcome aboard. Grab a chair."

They sat down and Jordan looked from Daniel to Jason. "So, are you guys, like, bonding?"

"I don't know." Daniel turned to Jason. "Are we?"

Jason shrugged as he started the motor. "Sure. Why not?"

"I think you have to hug," Jordan said.

Daniel's brow furrowed and he looked at Jason. "We don't have to hug, do we?"

Jason laughed. "Hell, no. We just have to catch fish."

CHAPTER FIFTEEN

SYDNEY PACED in front of the kitchen window, watching the cove for any sign of Jason's boat. "Do you think they're okay? They've been gone a long time."

Angie fed April the last few bites from a jar of mixed fruit. "If you're worried about Daniel, I'm sure Jason won't hurt him too badly. Of course, if you need to dispose of a body, the ocean is a pretty good place."

"That's not funny," Sydney said. Jason had been furious last night. Not that she thought he would actually hurt Daniel. At least, she hoped he wouldn't.

Angie blew out an exasperated breath. "Oh, hell, I can't stay mad at him. He's a doofus, but I love him to death. He has a good heart."

"'Morning," Lacey said shuffling into the kitchen. "Is there any coffee left?"

Sydney turned in her direction to reply and stopped dead, her mouth nearly falling open.

Gone were the colorful streaks in her hair, and the obnoxious makeup. Sydney had almost forgotten that Lacey's eyes were large and round like her own, not dark slashes in her face. She'd taken the ring out of her brow and had only two small stud earrings in each ear.

Sydney wanted to tell Lacey how great she looked, but she was afraid she might jinx it.

"There a little left in the pot," Angie said, her eyes also fixed on Lacey.

"What are you two staring at?" Lacey asked, obviously enjoying the shock value.

"Did you do something different with your hair?" Angie asked casually, pouring Lacey the last of the coffee.

Lacey took the cup and spooned sugar into it. "You guys are weird. Has anyone seen Jordan?"

"In his room asleep." Angie pointed her spoon at Sydney. "Hey, you think maybe they got lost in the Bermuda Triangle?"

Lacey rolled her eyes—her big, beautiful eyes. "The triangle is in the Atlantic Ocean between Miami, Bermuda and Puerto Rico. And Jordan isn't in his room."

Angie frowned. "He's not?"

As if on cue, Sydney heard the sound of a boat engine.

Angie looked out the window. "They're back. And Jordan is with them."

Sydney moved next to Angie and peered out. Jordan was tying the boat to the dock. Jason hopped out next, then Daniel—in one piece, thank God. As a matter of fact, they all looked…happy?

"Is it my imagination or are they smiling?" Sydney asked.

The three men walked up the beach to the porch. Jason was first through the door.

"Good morning, ladies." He tipped his baseball cap at Sydney and Lacey, and kissed Angie.

She wrinkled her nose and frowned. "Have you been *smoking?*"

Daniel and Jordan followed him inside.

"Where have you been?" Sydney asked.

"We went fishing," Daniel said.

Hearing his voice, April squealed and banged the high chair tray until he came over and dropped a kiss on the top of her rumpled head. "G'morning, munchkin."

"If you went fishing, where are the fish?" Angie asked.

"We didn't catch any," Jordan said. "We mostly just talked about sports. It was a male bonding thing."

Male bonding? Last night Jason and Daniel had wanted to hurt each other.

Angie looked from her brother to her fiancé. "So, you two are good now?"

Daniel looked at Jason. They both shrugged and Jason said. "Yeah, we're good."

"Oh, and by the way," Daniel said, walking over to Angie. He pulled her into his arms and hugged her hard. "I'm sorry."

She kissed his cheek. "You know I can't stay mad at you."

Sydney glanced over at Lacey and realized she was gazing up at Jordan with the biggest doe eyes Sydney had even seen, and Jordan was smiling back at her.

Huh?

When had they stopped wanting to zap each other off of the planet?

Jordan gestured toward the door and Lacey, without

taking her eyes off of him, said, "Mom, we're going for a walk."

Jordan took her hand and they stepped onto the porch. Eyes wide, Angie asked, "What the hell was that? I thought they hated each other."

"Who called it?" Daniel said, sounding proud of himself.

"Called what?" Jason asked.

"He thought that they were pretending they didn't like each other, because they actually *did* like each other," Angie said.

"Hell, I knew that," Jason said, and Angie gave him a playful shove.

"Who wants breakfast?" she said.

Sydney and Angie made everyone a pancake breakfast. Afterward the kids went down to the beach for a swim, while the adults lounged on the porch, drank iced coffee and chatted. It was a perfect day. Sunny and warm with a gentle breeze blowing off the ocean. Sydney wished they could stay another night, but everyone had to work Monday, so around four they packed up the van and piled in. This time Lacey and Jordan sat cuddled together in the corner, and every now and then out of the corner of her eye, Sydney saw them sneak a kiss.

"Is that not the sweetest thing you've ever seen?" Angie leaned forward to whisper.

"They do make a cute couple," Sydney whispered back.

Daniel, looking puzzled, asked, "When did her hair stop being green?"

When they got home Angie gave Sydney a big hug and said, "Thanks for coming with us. I loved having you there."

"I had a great time."

"We're going to do a girls' night out soon. Me and you and my sisters. Dinner and a movie."

Sydney tried to recall the last time she'd been out with the girls, but found she couldn't remember. "Sounds like fun."

Lacey and Jordan said a long, lingering goodbye, as if they wouldn't be seeing each other for a month, when in reality they would be reunited the next morning at work. And not five minutes after she finished unpacking, Lacey was calling him on her cell phone.

Sydney unpacked, and was on her way out the door to Daniel's when the home phone started to ring. When she saw Jeff's number she almost didn't answer it, but she saw on the caller ID that he'd called several times while they were gone, so this must be important.

The first words out of his mouth when she picked up were, "Where the hell have you been?"

Normally that would have annoyed the hell out of her, but Sydney had had such a fun weekend, nothing could spoil her good mood.

"We went away for the weekend," she told him.

"Without telling me? With *my* daughter," he snapped.

"Yes."

Her calm disposition seemed to infuriate him. "Where did you go?"

"Away with friends," she said.

"Friends? You mean your *boyfriend*."

"He was there."

"And you think that's an appropriate atmosphere for our daughter?"

"Yes, I do."

Her answer must have stunned him, because it took him a full ten seconds to respond. "I'm disappointed in you, Sydney. And you leave me no choice. I'm calling my lawyer in the morning and I'm going to file for sole custody."

As if she hadn't heard that tired old threat a dozen times before. "You go ahead and do that."

"You don't think I will?"

"Frankly, I don't care either way."

"Oh, I see. Now that you have a boyfriend, you don't want your daughter around?"

"Lacey is almost sixteen, Jeff. Do you honestly think a judge is going to change the custody order without talking to her first? And what do you suppose she'll say? That she'd love to go live with her dad and his girlfriend, the one he was screwing while he was still married to her mother? I'm sure she won't tell the judge what a horrible, humiliating experience it was to have the whole town know her family's business. So you go ahead and file for full custody."

"You're turning her against me," he said.

"No, you've done that all by yourself. Now, I have to go. I've got a date with my boyfriend." A boyfriend who cared about her feelings and treated her a damn sight better than Jeff ever had. And because of that, because of his decency, in the short time she had known Daniel, she'd come to care more about him, come to love him more, than she'd ever loved Jeff.

She was tempted to tell Jeff that, but he wasn't even worth the breath she'd have to expend. She hung up instead.

THE NEXT SIX WEEKS were more wonderful, more *perfect,* than Sydney could have ever hoped for. So wonderful and perfect, in fact, that she couldn't help wondering when the other shoe was going to drop. And when it finally did, it wasn't just one shoe. It felt like an entire closetful.

Her period was late.

She was sure it was fluke. She hadn't had a late period in four years, since she started taking birth control pills. And the fact that she was *on* the pill should have made getting pregnant impossible. Right?

But her period should have started on Tuesday, and now it was Friday and she hadn't so much as had a cramp. She didn't honestly think she could be pregnant, but she decided that taking a test, and seeing the negative result, would give her the reassurance she needed.

And if it wasn't negative? There was no point in even considering that, because it wasn't a possibility.

Daniel was working the afternoon shift, so after he left for work she packed April in the van and they took a trip to the store. She needed groceries anyway, so why not kill two birds, right? There were a dozen different brands of test, so she chose the most expensive, thinking it would be the most reliable, and grabbed a second, just in case the first was defective.

Back at her house, Sydney set April in her ExerSaucer, then carried in the groceries and put them away. She felt weird taking the test at Daniel's house. With her luck he would stop by and catch her in the act. Which would undoubtedly freak him out, even if it did turn out negative.

So she dragged the ExerSaucer into the hallway outside the bathroom, so she could keep an eye on April, then she sat on the edge of the toilet and read the directions thoroughly. Twice. Then, following them to the letter, she took the test.

Even though she was sure she wasn't pregnant, the next three minutes were among the longest of her life. *Pregnant* or *not pregnant*. She watched the seconds tick by, and when the three minutes were up she took a deep breath and turned it over.

Oh, shit.

Pregnant.

No, that couldn't be right. She was on the pill. There was no way she could be pregnant. She grabbed the second test and ripped open the plastic.

This time the three minutes took an *eternity*. She picked up the test with a trembling hand.

Shit.

Another positive.

No. This could *not* be happening. Then she had a thought. Maybe being on the pill could cause a false positive. Didn't it make a woman's body think it was pregnant?

That made perfect sense.

She heard the front door open, and Lacey called out.

Sydney grabbed the test wands and stuck them back in the box, which she then shoved into the cabinet under the sink.

"Why are you in this bathroom?" Lacey asked from the doorway.

"Straightening up," she lied, pulling herself to her feet. "Why are you home so early?"

"Early? It's almost six." She nodded to Sydney's shorts and tank. "Is that what you're wearing?"

"Wearing?"

"To the movie. Angie said she would be here at six-thirty to get pick you up."

Oh, hell. She had completely forgotten she and Angie were having a girls' night out and Lacey and Jordan were watching April. Dinner and a movie was the last thing she wanted to do right now. But she couldn't cancel on such short notice.

"I need to get in the shower," Lacey said. "I'm all sweaty from work."

"Sure, of course," Sydney said, stepping out into the hall, hoping Lacey wouldn't look under the sink.

"Are you okay?" Lacey asked. "You seem...nervous."

"No, I'm just...it's been a busy day."

"Okay, well, I'll be out in a few minutes."

It was too late to call the doctor's office, so Sydney grabbed April, went into the den and booted up the computer. She did an internet search on "birth control pills" and "false positive pregnancy tests." The more she read, the lower her heart sank. According to every source, there was nothing in birth control pills that could cause a false positive.

Meaning the odds were pretty good that she was pregnant.

She erased the search history and, feeling oddly numb, forced herself to go to her room and change, wondering how she was going to tell Daniel. How would he react? He already had one baby that he hadn't planned for. And she knew he didn't want to get married. Not yet, anyway. She honestly believed that they would be a family eventually, but after only a couple of months? She didn't think Daniel was even close to being ready for such a permanent commitment.

Sydney didn't need more time to know that she would be happy spending the rest of her life with him. And although it came as a shock, she wanted this baby. She loved Daniel. And though he had never said it, there was a chance he loved her, too.

And really, there was no reason she had to tell him right away. Maybe first she should try to get a feel for his state of mind. Hint around about the future and see how he reacted. And if he reacted badly? If he didn't want her or the baby? She couldn't fool herself into thinking that wasn't a possibility. At least this time it was *his* baby. Though given the circumstances, she wasn't sure how much of a consolation that would be.

"ARE YOU *sure* YOU'RE OKAY?" Angie asked as they were driving home from the movie theater.

"I'm fine," Sydney assured her, for about the fifteenth time since dinner. She was trying to act as if everything was normal, but it was tough. All Angie talked about during the meal was her pregnancy, and the small wedding she and Jason were planning for next month. Sydney had only managed to choke down a few bites of her pasta, and all through the film her mind kept wandering. She imagined a dozen different scenarios of what Daniel's reaction would be when she broke the news, and the next thing she knew the credits were rolling.

"So what did you think of the movie?" Angie asked.

"It was really good," Sydney said, even though she couldn't recall more than a few minutes of the story.

"Wasn't it hilarious when Jane pushed Devon off the dock into the water?"

She nodded, forcing a smile. "Yeah, it was funny."

Angie glanced over at her. "That never happened, and the characters names were Joan and Dennis."

Busted. "I guess I was a little distracted."

"Did you and Danny have a fight? Did he do something stupid? Because if he did, I'll totally kick his ass for you."

"He hasn't done anything. In fact, he's been wonderful. Other than arguing about where we're going for dinner, we never fight. It's almost too good." That meant something, right?

"There's no such thing as too good. And I'm glad to hear it, because you're the best thing that's ever happened to him."

Sydney just hoped Daniel felt the same way. But if he wasn't ready to get married yet, that was okay. There was no reason she and Daniel couldn't just live together, and raise April and the baby. They could be a family without being married.

"Daniel hasn't mentioned finding April's family lately. Has the P.I. had any news?"

"No. It was all pretty much a dead end. There was a cousin, but she was in rehab. Needless to say, she was in no condition to take a baby. He's looking into adoption now."

"He's not seriously going to give her up? He can't."

"Well, he got information from a couple of different agencies, and they all told him they could place April with no problem. That was almost a month ago and he hasn't made any arrangements. He hasn't said he's keeping her, but he also hasn't said he isn't."

"What the hell is this?" Angie said. Sydney followed her gaze out the windshield. The street was dark, but up ahead, in front of either her or Daniel's house, several police cars sat with their lights flashing.

Her heart dropped. Her first thought was April. Could she have choked or gotten hurt somehow? She was into everything now that she was crawling.

"Where are the kids?" Angie asked.

"Daniel's house."

As they got closer it was clear that the cars were parked in front of Sydney's house, and she could see Lacey and Jordan standing on Daniel's porch. And Lacey was holding April.

"Look," Sydney said, pointing them out. "They're fine."

"Thank God," Angie said, parking across the street from Daniel's house. They got out and Sydney could see that there was someone in the back of one of the patrol cars.

What the heck was going on?

"Sydney!"

She turned and saw Daniel, still in uniform, walking toward them from the side door.

"What's going on?" she asked him.

"Mom!" Lacey said, jogging up to her, April bouncing happily in her arms. Jordan was right behind her. "You are not going to believe what happened!"

"First, is everyone okay?" Angie asked, taking April from Lacey, looking her over thoroughly.

"Everyone is fine," Daniel assured her.

"Fred, Dad's gross handyman, was here again," Lacey said. "He grabbed me. But it's okay because Jordan punched his lights out."

Sydney's heart stalled. "What happened?"

"We were at Daniel's watching TV and we decided we wanted to watch the X-Men movie, so I came home to get it. I was unlocking the door and someone grabbed my arm. Then suddenly Jordan was there and he punched him."

"I was watching out the window," Jordan said. "It was dark, but I thought I saw someone sneaking around the house. I got there just as he grabbed her."

"And you punched him?" Angie said.

Jordan shrugged. "What else could I do?"

"He knocked him out cold with one punch," Daniel said, sounding proud of his nephew. Sydney was just relieved he'd been there to watch over her daughter.

"I think he's been following me around," Lacey said.

Sydney frowned. "What do you mean?"

"It seems like I've been seeing him everywhere lately."

"Why didn't you say something?"

"He never looks at me or talks to me, so I just figured it was a coincidence. I guess not. I told you he was a creep."

And Jeff thought Fred was harmless. She hoped he felt rotten when he learned what happened. Although, knowing Jeff, he would find a way to blame it on someone else. But Sydney was glad she listened to her instincts and changed the locks.

Jon Montgomery walked up to them.

"Hey, Angie. Hey, Syd," he said before turning to Daniel. "We're finished here. I'm going to take him in."

"I'll meet you there in a few minutes," Daniel said, then told Sydney and Angie, "Let's go inside."

They went over to Sydney's side door and gathered in the living room. Lacey must have gone in at some point because the lights were on.

"So, what happened after Jordan knocked this guy out?" Angie asked, sitting in an armchair with April. Lacey and Jordan sat on the couch.

"Jordan called me and I came right over," Daniel said. "Fred was just starting to come around when I pulled up."

"If you'll excuse me," Angie said, handing April to Lacey. "I don't want to miss anything, but I have a baby on my bladder. If I don't use your bathroom I'm going to wet myself."

"Go," Daniel said, waving her away.

"I want a restraining order against him," Sydney said. "I don't want him anywhere near my daughter."

"I think that's a good idea," Daniel said. "And I think an assault charge will stick if Lacey files a formal report."

"Does she have to do that tonight?"

"It can wait a day or two. Jon took her statement."

"And if we get a restraining order and Fred still bothers her?"

"California has pretty stiff anti-stalking laws. We'll keep him away from Lacey."

"We have a problem," Angie said coming back into the room. Everyone turned to look at her.

"What now?" Daniel asked.

"Look what I found on the bathroom counter." She was holding the pregnancy test box in one hand, and the wands in the other. "They're both positive."

How had they gotten on the bathroom counter?

"I'm sorry, Mom," Lacey said, looking mortified, her cheeks bright red. "I wanted to talk to you about it. That's why I left them out. I didn't think anyone else would see them."

"Jordan, I taught you better than this." Angie said, and the poor kid went white.

He stared at Lacey, then at his mom and said, "B-but, we haven't even had sex."

Well, that was good to know, although Sydney would have preferred not to find out quite like this.

"Angie, Lacey isn't pregnant," she said.

Clearly confused, Angie said, "But she said she put them there."

"I hid them under the sink, she found them and took them out."

"*Syd?*" Daniel said, now as pale as Jordan. There was no doubt *he* knew exactly what was going on.

This was not the way she'd intended to handle this.

Angie slapped a hand over her mouth. "Oh, my God, Sydney, I am so sorry. I thought…if I had known—"

"It's okay," Sydney said. But considering Daniel's shell-shocked expression, things were far from okay.

He was surprised. That's all. She just needed to give him a minute, to let it soak in. He would be fine after that.

"Lacey, Jordan," Angie said, setting the tests and boxes on the coffee table, "Why don't we go next door and put April to bed."

"Mom?" Lacey said, looking wary.

"Go ahead, honey. We'll talk later."

When they were gone Daniel reached out and picked up one of the tests, as if he had to see for himself.

He stared at it for a second, shaking his head, then he looked up at her and said, "What the hell, Sydney? How did this happen?"

"I don't know."

"You said you were on the pill."

"I was. I *am*."

"Did you miss a day? Forget to take it?"

She shook her head. "Never."

"Then how the *hell* did this happen?"

He was definitely not okay with this. He was nowhere near *okay*.

"I told you, I don't know how it happened. It just… did."

"I don't want kids."

"I know."

"You said all you wanted was *fun*."

"I remember what I said."

"What am I supposed to do now? Huh? *Marry* you? I don't want to marry *anyone*."

"Then you'll be happy to hear that I don't want to marry you, either." Why would she want to marry someone who didn't want her? Sydney had lived through that hell already. Definitely not a mistake she cared to repeat.

"I should have known this was too good to be true," he said. "I should have known there would be a catch."

"You say that like I did this on purpose."

"Did you?"

If he'd struck her, if he'd slapped her across the face, it couldn't have stung more. If Daniel thought that she was capable of something that underhanded and deceitful, he obviously didn't know her at all. And he sure wasn't the man she'd thought he was.

"Please leave," she said.

Those words, barely louder than a whisper, seemed to surprise him. He blinked, then opened his mouth as if he was about to say something, then closed it again. Then he did what she asked and left.

Feeling as if her legs might give out, Sydney sat on the couch. There was a pain in her chest, in her heart, so sharp and all-encompassing she found it difficult to breathe.

It was over. Just like that.

She heard a soft knock on the side door, and felt a glimmer of hope that maybe Daniel had come back. Maybe he wanted to at least say he was sorry. But it was Angie.

"Hey, you okay?"

"No. Not really."

"Sydney, I am so sorry. I never even considered that those might be yours."

"It's okay, Angie." If she had told him tonight, or next month, or three months from now, his reaction would have been the same. He didn't want a baby. And he didn't want a wife.

"He was upset?"

"You could say that."

"He was just surprised. You guys are going to be okay."

"No, we won't." The way Sydney felt right now, she would never be okay again.

CHAPTER SIXTEEN

W HEN D ANIEL pulled into his driveway an hour later, Angie's car was still parked across the street. Sydney's house was dark.

He shut the engine off and sat there for a minute, not looking forward to going inside and having to hear about what a shit he'd been. He was already clear on that fact.

What he didn't understand was Sydney's reaction. Why didn't she tell him he was being a jerk? Why did she just stand there and let him push her away? Why didn't she... *fight?*

He looked at his front window and sighed. Might as well get this over with.

He crossed the lawn to the front door and let himself in. Angie was on the couch with her feet propped on the coffee table, watching TV. When he stepped inside she switched it off.

"April just had a bottle and she's out. The kids left pizza in the fridge." She grabbed her purse and fished out her keys, then stood. "I'll see you later."

She started to walk toward the door.

Wait, that was *it?* "You're not going to lecture me on what a bastard I am?"

She stopped and turned. "I think everyone is pretty clear about that."

Touché.

Angie stood there, obviously unwilling to divulge anything without making him ask for it. "Did you talk to Sydney?"

"Yes."

"What did she say?"

His sister folded her arms. "Not much. I did most of the talking."

"Was she mad?"

"No. I don't know what you said to her, but it worked."

"What do you mean?"

"You've pushed her away. She is...*done*."

"Done with what?"

"*You,* Danny." Angie shook her head, eyes filled not with anger or disappointment, but with pity. "You're alone again. But that's the way you like it. Right?"

With that she turned and walked out. What the hell was with everyone tonight? Why wasn't she calling him names and telling him what a huge mistake he'd made?

And he didn't believe Sydney would really write him off. He was the father of her child, for God's sake. Yeah, he'd overreacted. And insinuating that she'd done it on purpose was definitely not one of his finer moments. He obviously hadn't meant it. And she was entitled to be furious with him, but she would cool off and they would talk about this and figure something out.

And the only reason he'd reacted the way he had

was that as soon as he'd figured out the tests were hers and not Lacey's, he'd imagined him and Sydney, with Lacey, April and the baby, together as a family. And how happy they could be. And it had scared the living shit out of him. That had *never* been part of the plan. But now, somehow, it just…made sense. He was used to having her around. He *liked* having her around.

Which was probably why he was so determined to make her think he didn't.

Which he knew made no sense at all. But old habits were hard to break. He wasn't accustomed to letting people in. Or keeping them around.

Sydney was going to have to understand that it would take time. If they were going to make this work, they would have to take things slowly. Maybe they could live together for a while, and if that worked, then they could talk about getting married.

Maybe.

Since Daniel knew Sydney wouldn't come to him, he swallowed his pride the following morning and went to her. He owed her that much. But the second she answered the door, he could see what Angie meant. She didn't smile, didn't frown, she didn't look angry or upset. Her face wasn't red and puffy, as if she'd been crying.

She didn't betray any emotion at all, and it made him nervous.

"Can we talk?" he asked.

"There's nothing more to say. You were pretty clear about your feelings last night."

Yeah, he deserved that, although he didn't think she

was trying to hurt him or make him feel guilty. "Please, just for a minute."

She moved aside so he could step in.

"April is taking a nap," he said, even though she hadn't asked. He tapped the monitor receiver that was clipped to his belt. "I'll hear her if she wakes up."

No smile, no shrug. She just stared up at him, that nothingness in her eyes.

"I wanted to say that last night, I reacted...badly."

She didn't confirm or deny it, didn't say anything at all.

"The thing is, I'm really sorry for the way I behaved. When I insinuated that you did it on purpose, I didn't mean it."

Nothing. No reaction. She could have had the decency to swear at him, or tell him to take his apology and shove it.

He started to get a very bad feeling.

"Sydney, would you please say something?"

"What would you like me to say?"

"Something. Anything. You could acknowledge that I'm talking to you."

"I hear you."

"But you have no comment?"

"I'm not sure what you expect me to say."

"I want to make this work, Sydney."

She frowned. Finally some sign that she wasn't an empty shell. "Why?"

"Because...I do."

"But *why?*"

Daniel didn't know how to answer that. He knew

exactly *why,* but couldn't put it into words. "Because...
we're supposed to be together."

"Supposed to be together?"

"Yes."

"You and me."

"Yes."

"The man who was in my living room last night, I
don't even know who he was. And I have no idea what
you wanted me to do. Scream at you? Throw things?
Maybe that worked for your parents, but that isn't
me."

That hurt. Badly. All his life he had wanted to be
anything but like his parents. But he had been a jerk
last night. Instead of trying to talk it through he'd overreacted and he'd expected her to play along.

That was the last time it would ever happen. "The
man in your living room last night was not me."

"You know what they say. If it looks like a giraffe,
and walks like a giraffe..."

Through the monitor, he heard April start to cry.

"You should go get her," she said.

"Come with me. We'll talk."

"There's really nothing left to say."

"Sydney, please."

She held the door open. "Goodbye."

Daniel had a million things he wanted to say to her,
if he could make her listen. And if there *was* a way, he
sure as hell didn't know how. She had obviously made
up her mind.

Angie had been right. Sydney was *done.*

And he'd been home five minutes before he realized

that leaving, not staying and fighting, was without a doubt one of his stupidest moves yet. And suddenly he knew exactly what he wanted to say.

What he should have said a long time ago.

DANIEL SERIOUSLY did not know when to quit.

Sydney thought she'd made herself pretty darned clear. And it had taken every ounce of strength she possessed not to break down, not to throw herself into his arms and tell him she loved him. But what would be the point? He wanted her now because he knew he couldn't have her anymore. Or maybe it was the same overdeveloped sense of responsibility that had motivated him to take April in. He felt compelled to do right by his child.

Whatever the reason, he was back at her door an hour later. This time carrying April. And this time he didn't ask if they could talk, or wait for her to step aside. He simply waltzed right in.

And for a second she just stood there, unsure of what to do. He was obviously having trouble with the whole breaking-up concept.

He walked through the kitchen and disappeared into the living room. She was about to follow him, when he returned carrying the ExerSaucer. He set it by the kitchen table and put April in it. "Talking may now commence," he said.

Who said she wanted to talk? Hadn't she already said that she was done talking?

"Should I start?" he asked, almost…cheerfully.

There was something very different about him. He

wasn't the repentant, remorseful man he'd been an hour ago. The one who didn't have a clue what he wanted or why. Only that he wanted *something*.

This guy *knew,* and it was making her uneasy. He'd blown it. He didn't deserve a second chance.

Sydney turned her back to him, leaning on the counter and looking out the window. "I don't want to talk to you."

"Is this what you did to Jeff? You froze him out? Is that what your mom did to you?"

She spun around.

He shrugged. "Hey, if you get to play the family dysfunction card, so do I."

She hated that he was right. That was exactly what her mother used to do. When she couldn't cope, she shut down. And yes, Sydney had probably done the same thing to Jeff. But her mother had an excuse. She was clinically depressed.

Sydney was fairly well-balanced, all things considered.

Daniel took a step toward her and she took one back, colliding with the edge of the counter. And she had that peculiar feeling again, like the first time he'd been in her kitchen. He was too...big. He was gobbling up all the air in the room.

"This isn't going to work, Daniel. I can't be with someone who freaks out every time things get a little stressful."

"And I can't be with someone who shuts down every time I freak out."

Uh, hadn't he just proved her point?

"And right now you're thinking that I just proved your point."

She blinked.

He took another step toward her. "But you're wrong." He paused, and when she didn't speak he said, "This is the part when you ask me *why*."

Okay, she would play along. "Why?"

"Because we're supposed to be together."

He took yet another step toward her, too close now. *Way* too close. She couldn't think straight.

"Ask me why," he said.

Like an obedient child, she asked, "Why?"

He propped his hands on the edge of the counter on either side of her, leaning in. "Because I love you. Because I want to marry you, have babies with you and spend the rest of my life with you."

Wow. For weeks she'd wanted to hear those words from him, but she never imagined him saying them with such feeling, with so much naked emotion in his eyes.

He wasn't telling her what he thought she wanted to hear. He meant every word.

He leaned in farther and kissed her so softly, so sweetly, that she felt herself melt. There was no way she could stay mad at him now. "In case you weren't sure," he whispered, pressing his forehead to hers, "this is the part where you tell me you love me, too."

"I do. I love you, Daniel." She closed her eyes and smiled. After keeping it bottled up inside for so long, it felt good to finally say the words. "I've wanted to say that for a really long time."

He pulled back a little so he could look at her, reached

up and touched her cheek. "I'm not going to lie to you. The idea of forever still scares me. But the idea of losing you? That *terrifies* me."

"And April?"

He looked over at the baby, bouncing in her seat, babbling at the toys, and smiled. "She managed to turn my entire life upside down. But I couldn't love her more if she were my own flesh and blood. She's my daughter. Although she figured that out a long time before I did."

Sydney wrapped her arms around him. "I never really believed you would give her up."

"Deep down I don't think I did, either. And I'll bet she's going to be an *awesome* big sister."

She smiled against his chest and hugged him tighter.

"I'm really sorry, Sydney, for the way I acted. I seem to have this knack for ruining what should be happy, tender moments."

"I actually never expected you to be happy about it. I hoped, but I didn't expect."

"Are you saying that I exceeded your expectations?"

She laughed. "I guess that's one way to look at it."

He lifted her chin, so he could look at her. "I'm happy now. I've been happy ever since you backed into my car and I made you nervous as hell. I knew there was something special about you."

"I'm happy, too." In fact, Sydney hadn't known it was possible to be this happy. She hugged him tight again, unable to let go just yet, and glanced over at the wall beside the door. That ridiculous hole was still there. She'd gotten so used to it, she barely noticed anymore. But she was glad it was there. It had become a symbol, a reminder that not so long ago her life had reached an all-time low, and here she was now, the happiest she'd ever been.

Funny how that worked. And she wouldn't have it any other way.

* * * * *

You're Invited to a *Double* Baby Shower!
For: Sydney Valenzia & Baby Boys (yes, two!)
Angelica Parkman & Baby Boy and Girl
Time: 2:00 p.m.
Given by: The very proud (and slightly over-whelmed) Grandmother and Aunts.

Bring your favorite dish to pass and plan on having a lot of fun!

HARLEQUIN *Super Romance*®

COMING NEXT MONTH

Available February 8, 2011

#1686 THE LAST GOODBYE
Going Back
Sarah Mayberry

#1687 IN HIS GOOD HANDS
Summerside Stories
Joan Kilby

#1688 HIS WIFE FOR ONE NIGHT
Marriage of Inconvenience
Molly O'Keefe

#1689 TAKEN TO THE EDGE
Project Justice
Kara Lennox

#1690 MADDIE INHERITS A COWBOY
Home on the Ranch
Jeannie Watt

#1691 PROMISE TO A BOY
Suddenly a Parent
Mary Brady

HARLEQUIN®

A Romance

FOR EVERY MOOD™

Spotlight on

Classic

Quintessential, modern love stories
that are romance at its finest.

See the next page
to enjoy a sneak peek from
the Harlequin® Romance series.

*Harlequin Romance author Donna Alward is loved
for her gorgeous rancher heroes.*

*Meet Wyatt as he's confronted by both a precious
little pink bundle left on his doorstep and his neighbor Elli
who's going to show him the ropes....*

Introducing
PROUD RANCHER, PRECIOUS BUNDLE

THE SQUAWKING QUIETED as Elli picked the baby up, and
Wyatt turned around, trying hard to ignore the feelings of
inadequacy as Darcy immediately stopped fussing.

"Maybe she's uncomfortable. What do you think, sweetheart?" Elli turned her conversation to the baby.

"What do you think is wrong?" Wyatt asked, putting the
coffee pot back on the burner.

A strange look passed over Elli's face, one that looked
like guilt and panic. But it was gone quickly. "I couldn't
say," she replied.

"But you were so good with her this afternoon." Wyatt
put his hands on his hips.

"Lucky, that's all. I just...remembered a few things."
The same strange look flitted over her features once more.

Wyatt took the coffee to the table. "You fooled me. You
looked like you knew exactly what you were doing." So
much so that Wyatt had felt completely inept. A feeling he
despised. He was used to being the one in control.

Elli and Darcy walked the length of the kitchen and
back. After a few moments, she admitted, "I haven't really
cared for a baby before. The things I thought of were simply
things I'd heard about. Not from experience, Mr. Black."

Her chin jutted up, closing the subject but making him

want to ask the questions now pulsing through his mind. But then he remembered the old saying—*Don't look a gift horse in the mouth.* He'd benefit from whatever insight she had and be glad of it.

"I don't really know what babies need," he said. "I fed her, patted her back like you did, walked her to sleep, but every time I put her down…"

Wyatt almost groaned. Of course. He'd forgotten one important thing. He'd been so focused on getting the formula the right temperature that he'd forgotten to check her diaper. Not that he had any clue what to do there either.

Pulling calves and shoveling out stalls was far less intimidating than one tiny newborn.

"She's probably due for a diaper change, isn't she." He tried to sound nonchalant. This was a perfect opportunity. Elli must know how to change a diaper. He could simply watch her so he'd know better for the next time.

Instead, Elli came around the corner of the counter and placed Darcy back in his arms. "Here you go, Uncle Wyatt," she said lightly. "You get diaper duty. I'll fix the coffee. Cream and sugar?"

Oh boy, Wyatt thought, looking down into Darcy's pursed face, his smug plan blown to smithereens. He was in for it now.

Will sparks fly between Elli and Wyatt?

Find out in
PROUD RANCHER, PRECIOUS BUNDLE
Available February 2011 from Harlequin Romance

HREXP0211

Try these Healthy and Delicious Spring Rolls!

INGREDIENTS

2 packages rice-paper
spring roll wrappers
(20 wrappers)

1 cup grated carrot

¼ cup bean sprouts

1 cucumber, julienned

1 red bell pepper, without
stem and seeds, julienned

4 green onions
finely chopped—
use only the green part

DIRECTIONS

1. Soak one rice-paper wrapper
   in a large bowl of hot water
   until softened.

2. Place a pinch each of carrots,
   sprouts, cucumber, bell
   pepper and green onion on the
   wrapper toward the bottom
   third of the rice paper.

3. Fold ends in and roll tightly
   to enclose filling.

4. Repeat with remaining
   wrappers. Chill before
   serving.

Find this and many more delectable recipes
including the perfect dipping sauce in

ROMANTIC SUSPENSE

Sparked by Danger, Fueled by Passion.

NEW YORK TIMES BESTSELLING AUTHOR

RACHEL LEE

No Ordinary Hero

Strange noises...a woman's mysterious disappearance and a killer on the loose who's too close for comfort.

With no where else to turn, Delia Carmody looks to her aloof neighbour to help, only to discover that Mike Windwalker is no ordinary hero.

Available in February.
Wherever books are sold.

Visit Silhouette Books at www.eHarlequin.com

SRS27709R2

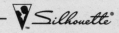

SPECIAL EDITION

FROM *USA TODAY* BESTSELLING AUTHOR
CHRISTINE RIMMER
COMES AN ALL-NEW BRAVO FAMILY TIES STORY.

Donovan McRae has experienced
the greatest loss a man can face, and
while he can't forgive himself, life—
and Abilene Bravo's love—are still
waiting for him. Can he find it in himself
to reach out and claim them?

Look for
DONOVAN'S CHILD
available February 2011